YOUR TRAINER SAYS HI

INDIE SPARKS

DEDICATION

This book is for everyone who ever trusted the wrong one and had to clean up the mess it caused in their life. Wick is the type of man who could make you forget the past ever happened. He gives good hot tub. He is good in so many other ways as well, but I repeat: He gives good hot tub.

Happy soaking! I meant that however you think I meant it.

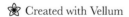

CONTENTS

ONE
BRUNCH WITH A TWIST

I look up from the table and watch my best friend walk into the restaurant. I'm not the only one who watches her. It's true what they say about happy people being more attractive. Oakley's always been gorgeous, but love looks really good on her.

"Are your feet even touching the ground? Come down already." I smile to make it clear I'm joking but I'm not sure I could offend her right now if I tried. She's in a bubble of bliss.

"What can I say, Nade? I had a *particularly* good morning." She winks, or Oakley's version of a wink, which requires facial contortions usually only seen in animation.

I roll my eyes but laugh while doing it. "Two years ago, you were desperately trying to convince everyone you weren't dating the guy. Now you wake up next to him every morning and still can't climb off his dick to be on time for brunch."

"Life is wild. Speaking of dicks, how's Heath? Has he sold enough powdered octopus sperm to be a millionaire yet?"

I snort mimosa out my nose, which is painful, by the way. "Ow, ow, ow." Thankfully, we're at the one place in town that still has paper napkin dispensers on the table instead of hoarding them in a secret location like they're made of gold.

"It's not octopus sperm; it's . . . fuck, I can never remember. Crab cartilage?"

"Jellyfish jizz?" She waggles her fingers, a motion I think is meant to symbolize the jellyfish themselves, not their little swimmers.

"That's probably right. How do you suppose you get a job jacking off jellyfish?"

Oakley shrugs. "You probably have to get naked in a pool with them and see how stiff their tentacles get."

"Or if they puff up at the sight of your clam." It's Oakley's turn to choke now. Champagne dribbles down her chin.

"Dammit, Nadine. Quit being funnier than me." She wipes her face. "But seriously, is that stuff selling?"

"No. It's just taking up space in his apartment. Heath wanted to ask corporate to add the whole line to our approved ingredient list so we could put it in smoothies. Like, what the fuck, dude? We're a franchise. We can't go rogue with the menu. The juice bar's brand is based on whole foods and fresh ingredients. Skweez is not going to let us promote some snake oil."

"Sea snake oil."

"Exactly. He's so into this crap all of a sudden. I think he genuinely believes he's going to make millions from it. He asked what I thought about him pitching it to Hollis."

Oakley's face freezes.

"Don't worry. I've already told him I'll light his balls on fire if he approaches your boyfriend with this. I'm just so shocked he's bought in to the hype and fallen for all the gilded promises they make about future income."

"Right? It's like you only knew him for six months before you went into business together or something."

I suck in a breath like I'm about to blow out a hundred birthday candles, but exhale too weakly to blow out a single match. "I know it was impulsive. But that was nearly a year ago and this franchise was a good opportunity. The juice bar itself is doing great. Heath and I agreed when we went into business together that if we didn't work out personally, we'd still be professional and run the store together. Honestly, I'd probably just let him buy me out. I still have my job."

"Has Heath ever had a real job?"

"Yeah, he worked for a marketing firm when we met. But right after we started dating, a couple startups he'd invested in paid off and he quit like he'd won the lottery. And then we bought the Skweez franchise. Now he tells people he's a venture capitalist, and claims his power lifting training and competitions require a flexible schedule."

"I'm just glad you kept your job."

"I would've never quit my job to open a juice bar. But I'm not sorry I went for it. It's making money." My phone lights up on the table next to my menu. "Speaking of . . ." I answer the call. "Hey, Paula." My accountant's voice on the other end is frantic. And Paula doesn't do frantic. Even by CPA standards, she's exceedingly stoic. I decipher the words she's spewing into my ear, and I know immediately there has been a mistake.

"No, that can't be right." Lowering my head to keep Oakley from reading my face, I try to keep my own tone calm and steady. "Let me look at the account and I'll call you back." My heart rate kicks up and a tremble spreads throughout my core. "We'll make payroll. Just give me a minute to see what's going on."

Without raising my head, I lower the phone to my lap, open my banking app, and navigate to our business accounts. The operating account is listed first and I can tell at a glance the balance is way too low. Something's definitely wrong. *Don't panic. There's probably a logical explanation.* Maybe some bill payments got doubled. Maybe someone else's debits accidentally posted to our account. Maybe a week's worth of our deposits is on hold. Any one of these things is technically possible, but a chaotic buzzing accelerates in my veins like I'm being invaded by hornets whose nest just got slapped with a broom. This tells me instinctively what I'm going to find when I scroll to the payroll account. I have a sixth sense for tragic fuckery.

There not only isn't enough money to pay our employees this week, the account is wiped out. Nineteen dollars, ninety-eight cents? That should be my brunch tab, not a business checking account balance.

My hands are in full quake-mode by the time my thumb smashes the call icon under Heath's name in my contacts. He barely gets "hello" out of his mouth before I say, "What. Have. You. Done?"

I make no mention of money at all, but it's clear he knows exactly what I'm asking as he indicts himself with the three little words that transmit guilt brighter than neon: "I can explain."

"You better be able to outrun me because if you're about to say what I think you're about to say, this is your last day on earth."

The next thing I know, Oakley has lunged across the table and is prying my white-knuckled fingers off a knife that I don't remember clutching, as she chants, "Oh, shit. Oh, shit. Oh, shit."

Once she has the knife freed and securely out of my immediate reach, she says, "I'll drive."

TWO

INSULT TO INJURY

"At least you don't live together," Oakley says as she rounds the corner out of the restaurant parking lot. "Believe me, that made my breakup with Christian so much more complicated."

She says it as though I wasn't around for the whole ordeal, which was not, in fact, all that complicated. What I'm dealing with right now seems a million times worse than having to find a new place to live. I'm not offended, though. This is what Oakley does when she's upset: she rambles, and sometimes, she doesn't exactly weigh the words before they come flying out of her mouth. She's a fixer, and she thinks she's helping. Honestly, I can't even hear what she's saying anymore. All I can hear is the grand idea Heath floated over dinner Saturday night . . .

I don't understand why we're not on the same page about this. It just makes so much sense for us to take the next step and move in together.

At the time, I chalked it up to him moving faster than me emotionally, not being able to help how hard he was falling for me, and a whole lot of other romantic bullshit I could kick myself for wanting to believe. I think I knew deep down, even then, that when he said it made sense, what he meant was if he didn't have to cover rent on his own anymore, he could buy up to the next level of his new side hustle. He'd mentioned the investment opportunity so many times I'd starting tuning it out weeks ago.

He was obsessive to the point it seemed like a passing phase approaching its pinnacle, like when my little brother was incessantly filling binders full of Pokémon cards. Or when I was so obsessed with jelly bracelets that I couldn't leave the house without both forearms covered in them. But we were kids. It's normal for kids to get carried away with new things. It's part of growing up. Heath is a full-grown man.

And I am a full-grown woman, who should've known better. *Fuuuuuuuck!*

This all happened so fast. One day he was showing a slight interest in this weird supplement company, and the next, he was a brochure-thumping disciple, spreading the gospel of the micro-nutritional secrets of the deep seas.

I'm sure his rent money went into the scam, too. It probably already had by the time he clinked his wine glass to mine and proposed our cohabitation.

Oakley turns the wheel again and I realize she's headed for my bank. "No," I say. "I need to confront Heath first. He's at his apartment." I hold up my phone to validate my confidence. "We share our locations."

She shakes her head hard, her lashes fluttering as she rolls her eyes. She's exasperated with me—and that's my role in this friendship, so now I'm really pissed. I'm the logical one, the voice of reason, the one people turn to when they want the unvarnished truth. I've never been the one who needed someone else to take the wheel, literally or figuratively. My anger swells with every breath I take.

"I need to see him right now while my rage is still fresh. He should have to face me and account for this in person!"

My best friend's tone is sharp-edged enough to cut through my need for vengeance when she says, "No. You need to take care of the financial stuff before you deal with him. People are counting on getting paid on Friday and if they don't, you'll be facing far bigger problems, Nade. Real shit first, bullshit second."

Goddammit! Real shit first, bullshit second is my line. "Fine. I'll get payroll sorted first. But then I'm going to peel his face off his skull like a sausage casing."

She fakes a dry-heave as she angles into a parking spot. "That is so disturbing I'm going to pretend you didn't even say it."

Oakley sits patiently in a scratchy orange chair in the lobby while I meet with a banking specialist in a glass-walled cubicle. It's like being in a human fishbowl. I've been here before but always when I was riding a wave of pride and excitement—opening a new account, signing loan paperwork —but today, I feel more like a beggar than a qualified customer. I'm hyper-aware of everyone walking past, the small movements of the people in the neighboring fishbowl as they shift in their seats, every button lighting up on the damn desktop phone in front of me. The desire to smash that hunk of blinking plastic is strong.

This must be what people mean when they talk about sensory overload. I open and close my hands to stretch my fingers. My skin feels like it's shrinking on my body.

I've always been stubborn. I know this about myself, yet it still shocks me every time it doesn't serve me well. The signs were all there that something bad was brewing with Heath. But I just kept ignoring the discomfort and telling myself we were fine. We were never a good fit. He was charming. And I guess I needed to be charmed. Now, I need a loan to bail us both out of this mess he created.

Nicholas, the banking specialist seated across the desk from me, suddenly raises his eyebrows at his computer screen and goes, "Hmmmm. Alrighty then." His fingers tap dance across his keyboard.

"Is everything okay?" I ask. All the sounds and sights that were torturing me a few seconds ago become silent and invisible at once, but my nerves are still buzzing.

"Well . . ." he says, dragging out the end of the word. "I'm afraid your application has been denied. We are unable to increase your business line of credit at this time."

"Excuse me? I have perfect credit. I've never missed a payment on anything in my life. What's the problem?"

Nicholas sits taller in his chair. "Your average balances in your business accounts have dropped off significantly over the past few months, which can indicate some sudden financial instability. And your credit line has been maxed out for the past several billing cycles as well. That, too, poses an increase potential for risk."

"We intentionally applied for a lower line of credit than we could've qualified for, but now we need more. We misjudged. It's just growing pains. They're a necessary part of expanding a business."

"Right, and of course, we understand these things can happen." His voice is softer and slower now, like he's trying to dissuade a bomber from lighting the fuse. "That's precisely why we have the option of escalating your application. And based on your history with us and your excellent credit, I certainly feel comfortable doing that."

"Great. How long, will it take? I have an errand I could go run and come back."

Nicholas's shoulders sag a little, not for long before he stiffens his spine again, but that slump is unmistakable, and I know that's not good. Slumping is never good. "Our loan review board meets twice a month and, fortunately for you, they're meeting next Wednesday. Looks like you came in at a good time. I'll send this up this chain and—"

"I don't suppose there's any chance by *next* Wednesday, you meant tomorrow?"

"No, I'm afraid I mean the next one after that. Eight days from now."

"I can't wait eight days. I have to make payroll by Friday, which means the money has to be in the account by Thursday morning so we can make the transfer to the payroll processor. I don't think you understand how any of this works." I stand so I can think better. "I need to speak to someone else."

"There is no one else."

I look around incredulously, lifting and lowering my hands at my sides as if I'm gauging the weight of imaginary objects. "You do realize I can see all these other employees, right? I'm sure at least one of them has to outrank you, and that's the one I need to talk to!" I'm aware of the rising volume of my voice but sometimes yelling really does help, and I'm pretty sure this is one of those times. "Get me a manager!" *Fuck me. I can't believe I'm going to have to go full-Karen to get this done.*

He sighs but makes no move to stand. "I understand this is not the outcome you were expecting, Ms. Garrison, but if you'll sit back down, we can go over the additional items I'll need to complete your application."

"What additional items? It's complete."

"It's complete for automated review. In order for the loan board to review it, I'm going to need some further documentation, including recent paystubs, your tax returns for the past two years—"

Let the record show I tried to remain calm, but Nicholas is apparently choosing violence today. "You reviewed all of those things when we opened the business less than a year ago. No new returns have been filed yet. Nothing has changed!" My hands wrap around the phone on his desk and I pull to remove the slack from the cord. I sense Oakley standing from her scratchy orange chair. I swear I can feel her moving toward us, so I yank as hard as I can.

In my mind, the phone dramatically detaches from the wall in an epic show of *I Didn't Come Here To Play, Nicholas!* In reality, it remains connected and I trip over my own feet, nearly losing my balance. I try to brace myself on the chair I'd been sitting in earlier, completely forgetting it's on casters. The force of my weight pushing on the arm sends it into a spin, and the next thing I know, I've tied myself to it via a full revolution with the phone cord still in my hand.

In an attempt to demonstrate my take-no-prisoners mentality, I've taken myself prisoner. From the corner of my eye, I see the sun glinting off a silver badge. A slight turn of my head brings the officer fully into view as he enters the lobby. "You called the fucking cops? What the hell, Nicholas? Did you hit an alarm button or something? It's not like a pulled a gun on you!" Heads dart in our direction from the glass house next door.

Nicholas is on his feet now. "That police officer is a customer. And if you could please get a hold of yourself, we can let him do his banking without having to break out his handcuffs."

"Pfft. Handcuffs. You wish."

Oakley bursts into the fish bowl and grabs the phone. She circles the chair in the opposite direction to extricate me from the bondage of my own doing. "I'm so sorry," she apologizes on my behalf, setting the phone back on the desk. "It's been an incredibly hard morning. She's processing a lot right now. We're going."

"You send that application up that chain, Nicholas!" I yell as Oakley drags me over the threshold and back into the lobby. "I'll be back!"

"Not today, I promise," Oakley assures him with a nervous smile.

I break free of her grasp and storm out onto the sidewalk. "I don't need you to speak for me," I snap when she joins me.

"Trust me, you do. Get in the car."

"They denied the increase to our credit line because Heath took all the money from our accounts."

"Well, if he hadn't taken all the money, you wouldn't need the increase."

"That's what I said!"

"Okay, get in. I'll take you to his apartment. But you have to promise me you will stay a safe distance from Heath. And from the kitchen knives."

I slide in and buckle my seat belt.

"I'm not starting this car until you promise."

Internally, I shrug. "Jesus, Oakley! I'm not going to stab him." *But he better have that money or so help me, I am not responsible for any blade-free injuries he may suffer.*

THREE
SACRIFICIAL MUFFINS

The whole ride over to Heath's apartment, I've been silently reciting, "I will remain calm, cool, and collected." But the moment the tires stop spinning, that mantra explodes into a million tiny poison arrows, and I'm hellbent for his front door, ready to spit them all right at his stupid face.

To my surprise, my knuckles meet his front door with the cadence of someone who is indeed calm, cool, and collected. It's a very cordial knock. I'm not even shaking. Then he answers and the sight of his smile instantly releases the arrows. I shove the door, sending him off kilter as words fly from my mouth, scattershot and bloodthirsty.

"What the actual fuck were you thinking? Did you think I wouldn't notice? Were you under the impression a payroll fairy would swoop in and magically pay our employees? With what, Heath? Little vials of powdered shrimp shit? Where's the money?"

The smell of cinnamon wafts from his kitchen. "Are you . . . baking?"

"You're mad now, but once you hear what I've come up with, you're going to be proud. So, we can't put the supplement powders into our smoothies, right? Approved franchise ingredients . . . blah, blah, blah, whatever. Well, your genius boyfriend read the fine print, sweets. And guess what? There is no approved ingredient list for baked goods! Ha!" He claps his hands together, swiping them against each other, wiping flour onto the floor.

"That's probably because we don't own a bakery. We own a juice bar. A franchise that you've put in jeopardy. You know corporate reviews our financials. We are going to have to explain those withdrawals. Not to mention, replenish the accounts. Today!"

"Relax, sweets—"

"Call me *sweets* one more time and you'll be choking on your own teeth."

His eyes flit to the doorway and his brows lift. "Hey, Oakley. What are you doing here?"

"I drove her over here." She steps inside and pulls the door closed behind her. "Why else would I be at your door?"

"Oh, cool. Want a muffin? They're still warm."

Oakley's eyes meet mine and I'm momentarily grateful for a witness. "No," I say. "She does not want a muffin. I don't want a muffin. Nobody wants your stupid fucking muffins! What I do want is the money put back in the accounts. Do whatever it is you need to do to cancel your investment and get a refund."

"That money is multiplying as we speak." He lifts his fists in front of his face and flicks his fingers out like someone demonstrating fireworks exploding in the air. Small wisps of flour hang between us like thin smoke. "You're angry now, but when you see the return on our investment, you'll thank me for getting us in on the ground floor."

"I am never going to thank you for this. Thanks to you, I can't even get a loan to cover payroll! I'm going to have to pull from my personal savings. But you will repay me. With interest. Get that money back, and don't you dare take another penny out of our business accounts without consulting me."

"Well, I can't just get it back. That's not how it works."

"It doesn't work at all! It's a scam! How much did you give them?"

"Haven't you ever heard that you have to spend money to make money? For somebody with a business degree, you really don't have a very good head for it. I'm not trying to be mean, but damn. This is pretty basic shit, Nadine."

The room goes blurry but I distinctly hear Oakley murmur, "Oh, you poor, dumb bastard."

I can't describe what happens next in any vivid detail. All I know is there is a pile of crumbled cinnamon sea-smut muffins at my feet, and Heath has a dent in his forehead that seems to be the same thickness as the edge of the muffin pan now teetering on the top corner of the fridge. There's a matching pan spinning on the floor tiles. The one on the fridge clatters to the floor and I jump. Heath jumps. We all jump. Nothing about this is funny but a wave of maniacal laughter escapes me. He backs away from me in slow steps until he meets the countertop and there's nowhere else for him to go.

The room gets blurry again, but this time it's because of the tears filling my eyes. How is this my life? I'm smart. I'm accomplished. And I have a goddamn excellent head for business, thank you very much! So why am I standing here with my eyes leaking and a crust of cinnamon and sugar, and who knows what sort of powdered sea debris, caked under my fingernails while my oh-so-very-*ex*-boyfriend surveys me with the eyes of a terrified animal, and my best friend stands by in ready-to-launch mode?

How did he even become my boyfriend? Look at him with his bulging muscles, as if he's so strong. His skittish eyes and that weak chin he thinks he's hiding behind that thin goatee tell a more accurate story.

He has no idea why I'm this angry. He really is that fucking dumb. And he's not just my ex-boyfriend, he's my business partner. I groan like a wounded animal. The death knell of my dignity. I have never been more ashamed of my own choices.

"We are done on a personal level. We have no choice but to work together until I can figure out how best to handle this from a legal standpoint. I think it would be best if we communicated through our attorneys for a while."

"I don't have an attorney," he says. "And I don't want us to break up. Why are you doing this?"

The dent in his forehead is getting deeper as the swelling grows around it. I assaulted him with bakeware and he thinks we should keep dating. My financial loss weighs heavier all of a sudden. "You handed that money over to a multi-level-marketing company without even having an attorney read the contract? Not that it would've been worth the paper it was printed on, but at least I could've kept believing you had an ounce of sense if you'd exercised some degree of caution! This isn't the same as the investments you made before, Heath."

"I didn't need an attorney to read a one-page contract."

"A one-page contract?"

"Not a full page even. Bounty of the Seas operates on the premise that just as the seas are unquantifiable, so should our belief in our possibilities be. The contract literally just says we are giving in good faith with the belief of exponential return based on our own efforts. You gotta believe to achieve. There's power in manifestation. If you'd watch the videos with me, you'd get it. I know you would."

"You literally signed a piece of paper confirming the money was a gift?"

"It's not a gift. It's an investment. In myself. In us. Our future. I don't understand why you refuse to give this a chance. The risk tolerance isn't even that high once you read the clinical studies. I have all the numbers. You've seen the brochures!"

My eyes land on a bag of the mystery supplement powder

on his counter and the visual of the logo rocks me to my core. Bounty of the Seas. "Their acronym is BOTS, Heath. It's like a cruel joke. That's exactly what they think of their followers, that you're a bunch of brainless bots."

"No, they don't. But they're not limited by traditional ways of thinking about money and wealth." He shakes his head. "I thought you were more open-minded, I guess."

"And I didn't realize you were a complete imbecile."

"An imbecile that makes you speak in tongues when mine's buried in your pussy."

"Nobody needs you for that. I can achieve that on my own with a couple double-A batteries and eight spare minutes. But for the record, you can only make me do that with your tongue on my clit, not in my pussy. The fact that you're not even clear on that particular order of operations makes me seriously doubt you have any clue at all what you signed!"

"Ohhh-kaaay!" Oakley steps between us. "I think we've all lost sight of the financial urgency at hand." She looks Heath up and down as if she can't quite believe he's real. By the time she turns her gaze to me, I'm resigned to the fact that I'm on my own to fix this problem. I'm on my own to fix all my problems. "Back to the bank?" she asks.

"I can make the transfer online."

"And we live to avoid jail for another day." Her smile is everything I need, equal parts strength and sarcasm. There's a truth in her eyes that lets me know she thinks I'm every bit as big an idiot as I feel right now, but she'd still testify under oath that Heath hit himself in the head with that muffin pan.

Before we leave, I step nose-to-nose with him. "I don't care what you have to sacrifice to make it happen, but you will repay the business. Cut your daily trips to the coffee shop, cut restaurants, cut your beloved personal trainer. Whatever it takes, however you make it happen, I expect payments to start soon."

"My personal trainer is paid quarterly and I just made a

payment last month, so giving up my sessions with Wick won't save any money. And before you even ask, it's nonrefundable."

"Interesting. See, what I just heard was that I have a personal trainer for the next few months. Good timing, too, because I've got a hell of a lot of frustrations to work off. Tell your boy to be ready for me."

Damn, that felt good. A broke bitch can still be a bad bitch.

But the mirror in his foyer reflects a sad bitch instead. *Yeah, I really need to start wearing waterproof mascara.*

Back in Oakley's passenger seat, I log into Heath's calendar before he remembers I have access and kicks me out. "Nice. He has an appointment with his trainer tomorrow morning. I'll be there."

"How do you know when his next appointment is?"

"I have access to his calendar because I always have to remind him of things."

"His calendar can send him reminders."

"He likes it better when I remind him because I add personal notes." *Oh, dear goddess. Please hurl me into a volcano for admitting that out loud.* "Don't say it. Please."

"I'll give you some time to recover emotionally. But don't think for a minute I'm not keeping track."

"Fair enough." I log into my banking app and take a deep breath as I send a chunk of my savings hurtling through cyberspace into the juice bar's payroll account. What's done is done.

"Nade, look at me." The last thing I want to do is look at Oakley right now. She's in the best place she's ever been. Her job's going great. Her relationship is goals. I cut my eyes up to see her in the exact moment the sun peaks from behind a downtown roofline, casting her in a near-angelic golden glow. "You are going to be just fine. It would take a hell of a lot more than that puffed-up weasel to take you out. You are Nadine Motherfucking Garrison."

"Only the best of friends share a middle name." I'm smiling on the inside but my face isn't having it.

"Yeah, and that muffin-making motherfucker better not forget it." She pounds her hand on the steering wheel. She's so fired up, and I love her for it. She may not have the mouth of an angel, but she's got the heart of a saint.

I open my own calendar and add my training session with Wick to tomorrow's agenda, and then I add Buy Waterproof Mascara.

FOUR
ZERO TO HORNY

I roll over and tell myself this day will be better. The birds are chirping, the sun is shining . . . and I'm already exhausted because I slept like shit. It's entirely too soon to be having sex dreams about my ex. Well, my most recent one, anyway. Why couldn't my subconscious cycle back a few years and give me a jog down memory lane that I could enjoy? The sex wasn't even great with Heath. It hasn't been great since . . . . before.

Monk-Monk, my three-foot-tall pink and purple monkey stares at me from the chair in the corner with his gangly limbs and his plastic eyes of disapproval. "Don't look at me like that." I pull the covers over my head.

Maybe if I went back to sleep, I'd have a better dream . . . no, I can't let myself hit the snooze button today. Heath is a morning person so, of course, he meets with his personal trainer at 7:00 a.m. One more red flag I ignored.

Not that I care about being at the top of my game for this training session. I'm only going because there's literally nothing else I can take from Heath that would matter. Not that co-opting his personal trainer is on par with what he's taken from me, but fitness is his passion. Well, it was before he got a taste of the jellyfish jizz, anyway.

I don't even like Wick. Okay, I don't really know him, but I know he's cocky. Totally full of himself in that gym-bro way. Heath and I go to the same gym. It's where we met but I'm not going to think about that today. I've only seen Wick from across the room, no interaction beyond a smile and a head nod, but that's plenty to know exactly who I'm going to be dealing with. I'm in sales. It's my job to read people. And I've got a definite read on this guy.

My body already hates me for dragging it out of bed right when the alarm went off like some kind of optimistic nutjob. There is not a muscle in my body that wants to work out this morning. It's a rare day with no meetings, no clients I have to call on. If not for this damn training session, I could've stayed in bed and wallowed in self-pity for a while.

But there's revenge to be had and I deserve to have it, so I'm on my feet. As I wiggle into my leggings, it's getting less and less clear how this plan is going to make anything about my current situation any better.

I give myself a lemonade-from-lemons pep talk in the bathroom mirror, but the face staring back reminds me I don't buy into all that rah-rah motivational crap. Sometimes life sucks, and it doesn't magically get better because you smile and envision butterflies and cotton candy. It gets better because you get the fuck up off the floor and make shit happen for yourself. *Get in the car, loser. We're going to the gym.*

Who knew this many masochists came to the gym so early? The parking lot is full, the locker room is full, and there is a body on every machine with at least one waiting. I hate them all.

Wick wasn't at the front desk when I came in. I don't see him loitering around the free weights, flexing and checking out all the spandex-clad female butts walking around like he usually does. He's definitely an ass man. I wander back up to the entrance, and there he is, so it looks like I'm really doing this. Show time. I stride confidently up to the counter. "Hey, I'm your seven o'clock."

He scrunches his forehead and gives me the *I don't think so* eyebrows. "Huh. Alright then. Let's get started." Just like that. He doesn't even question it. I guess anyone could walk in off the street and claim they're his next client and he'd just lead them down the hall like he's leading me right now.

Not that I'm complaining. I might be guilty of checking out an ass myself right now. His is definite eye candy in those coaching shorts. Nice glutes. And those leg muscles. Holy shit. When Oakley met Hollis, she wouldn't shut up about his great thighs. I thought it was a weird body part to be so impressed by, but um, yeah. Wow. My eyes roam up his narrowed waist. My breath hitches when my gaze reaches the expanse of his shoulders. He looks bigger than he used to.

I stop at the scale in the hallway but he keeps going. "Don't you need me to step on this before we begin?

"Why?"

"So you can record my weight. Isn't that part of the deal? We're going to be working together for the next couple months, by the way."

His stare is penetrating. "Come with me," he says, slowly, like someone set his audio output to a lower speed.

It takes a beat for my brain to correctly process that one. My first interpretation was purely sexual. Apparently, somebody's messed with my settings, too. What the hell? Wick is already five steps ahead by the time my legs decide to move. I walk quickly to catch up before he notices I'm not following him.

He leads me into an office and closes the door behind us. "Have a seat."

It's only after I'm sitting that I realize this is his second command I've followed. He sits on the opposite side of the desk. "Let's talk about your history."

"Or we could start with my name and why I'm here."

"I know your name. You're Nadine, Heath's girl. And I assume you're here because he gave you his session, which isn't allowed, by the way, but I don't really care. I'm logging the session under his name and not asking any questions about that. But I do have a few about you."

"First of all, I'm my own person, not *Heath's girl*. Second of all, I'm not his anything because we broke up."

"The plot thickens. But like I said, I don't care. However, if I'm going to work with you, I need to know something. I'm just going to cut to the chase here. Do you have an eating disorder, Nadine?"

"No, I do not." The chill in my voice is only matched by the ice his question has left in my veins.

"Are you sure? Because nutrition is a crucial part of train-ing. It's as important as the workouts." His eyes try to possess me again. "You're very thin, and your eagerness to check your weight is concerning."

My shoulders round and my gut churns. Every high school taunt and accusation rings out in my head. People have felt enti-tled to comment on my weight my entire life. To question it. *Why are you so skinny? How do you eat like you do and not gain weight? It's not natural. It's not fair. God, you're so lucky. Curves are sexy. Why don't you want them? Nobody likes a girl who's all skin and bones. You could get a boob job. Hey, we're setting up a fundraiser so you can get butt implants. Look, it says who wants to buy Nadine's ass? Hahahahahaha. It's obvious you have a problem. You're not fooling anyone. Tell me your secret.*

The only secret was how desperately I wanted to have a normal body, and to be able to join a conversation about girl-body stuff without being shut out like I had nothing to contribute. I didn't have discernible curves until my senior year of college. They're still practically invisible unless I'm wearing fabric that clings or I'm naked.

That nice hum Wick sparked in my body a few moments ago is now a burning pit of acid. He's zeroed in on my biggest weakness in less than five minutes. I knew he was an asshole. Fucking overgrown frat boy. "I've been unnaturally skinny my whole life, okay?"

"It's not unnatural if that's your body type without self-harm. If you eat a balanced diet and take care of yourself and you're naturally thin, that's fine. I just need to be sure I'm not going to be contributing to something harmful, Nadine. Training isn't just about burning calories."

Could he be any more condescending? Smug bastard. "If you wanted to analyze somebody with unhealthy obsessions, you should've turned that focus on Heath. He's the one with that problem, not me!"

"Whoa. I'm a personal trainer, not a trained mental health professional." He tosses the pen up and lets it fall to the desk. Leaning forward, he says, "Do you really want to work out today, or do you just need someone to talk to?"

"What do you care? Anyway, I have friends. I don't need to talk to one of Heath's."

"He and I aren't friends."

"That would be news to him. He practically worships you. He thinks every word out of your mouth about fitness and nutrition is the best advice in the world."

"Pretty sure your intel is outdated because I haven't seen Heath in weeks. Not since I refused to invest in that pyramid scheme he's all wrapped up in. Do you use that stuff, too?"

"Oh, okay, so I not only look too skinny, but also stupid. Got it."

His laugh is warm and his wintry eyes thaw as he relaxes.

"You do not look stupid. Or too skinny, but my clients' overall health matters to me."

My defenses melt a little. He seems sincere. And my god, he is absolutely beautiful, which makes it incredibly hard to hate him. Of course, that's exactly the type of advantage a conman would exploit to its full evil potential. Look where trust got me with the last guy. Nope. Not going there. "Let's try this again." I inhale to center myself and square my shoulders back where they belong. "No, I do not have an eating disorder, nor have I ever had one."

"Okay. Then let's hit the gym so I can check out your form—" He pauses and starts over. "I need to make sure you know how to properly use the equipment and that you practice the right postures to avoid injury. We can start with the fact that you don't know how to do a proper squat."

"Was that a hypothetical example of the type of thing you look for?"

"No. It's a fact. I've watched you and you don't know what you're doing. You may not get hurt doing them the way you do, but you're never going to see any real results."

Sir, how dare you appeal to my competitive nature like you've read my instruction manual! "Are you insinuating you could do great things for my ass?"

"Are you flirting with me?"

"That would be inappropriate."

"It would indeed. Much like the thoughts I'm currently having about your cute little ass."

"For someone who's so worried about integrity, this conversation seems to have taken quite the risky turn."

"What can I say? I've never met a challenge I didn't want to take."

The air between us is sizzling and I don't think I've ever gone from zero interest to raw lust so fast in my life. His eyes are all the way thawed now. And his wicked glimmer has my pussy all the way clenched. I should pump the brakes here. But that's not at all what I want to pump.

"Well, I guess we should hit the gym, like you said, so you can show me the error of my ways."

"You're going to hate me when we're done."

"Is that a promise?"

FIVE
TASTE TESTING

Wick made no false claims about the intensity of the workout he intended to put me though. And I have no regrets. I had no idea how badly I needed to push myself to my limit and sweat out the toxic bullshit I've allowed into my life.

Those corrections he made to my squat technique were no joke. Damn. No wonder everybody hates squats. I've spent all these years thinking I had them mastered, and if everyone would quit whining and learn to squat like me, they'd be fine. Yeah, that false sense of superiority has been completely obliterated. My ass is killing me, along with my quads. And my barely-there biceps, too. *Hello, spaghetti arms.* He put my whole body through it.

Seriously, it hurts to hold my arms up to wash my hair. But I could stand in this steamy shower all day if I didn't feel guilty about someone else needing it. Plus, I'm afraid if I don't keep moving, all my muscles might seize.

I don't have the strength to blow dry my hair. Towel-dried and into a ponytail it goes. Forget makeup. All I have to do today is return emails and authorize next week's produce order for the store. Shit. I'd forgotten about inventory, and the fact that Heath withdrew from the operating account, too. Guess I'll be making another transfer. I should've hit him with something way bigger than a muffin pan.

I'm convinced that CPAs are supposed to be a little scary, but Paula's advice about talking to an attorney plays on repeat in my head as I get dressed, and it gets more terrifying every time. There's no guarantee Heath would step aside without the store being sold. And I don't want to sell it.

I hate admitting professional failure of any sort, but this is a personal failure as well. I'd rather stand naked in a glass booth and let strangers critique my body. Almost.

Wick is at the front counter when I'm leaving, and when I look back to wave goodbye before I step out the door, I find him watching me. He smiles and says, "Do you hate me?"

"Nah, just a mild dislike." I shrug, despite the ache in my shoulders. "Nothing a nice long soak in bath of Epsom salt won't cure."

"Can't lie. I do love knowing I've left a woman sore."

My cheeks flame. He can't just blatantly say something that suggestive in a crowded gym, especially not in the lobby where nobody's even focused on their workout yet. No one else shows any reaction but there's no way we're the only two people who heard him. The arrogance. The audacity! His smile hasn't faded—if anything, it's wider now. So proud of himself for making me blush. I should be repulsed. So how come I'm not?

I can't concentrate in my home office. Driving in to the actual office sounds terrible, but I have to get out of here. It's too quiet, even with music on. My thoughts are chaotic, and I know the only thing that will keep me on task is the energy of other people moving and talking around me. The effort to tune out the distractions will shut down the intrusive thoughts.

Honestly, I work best when my focus is split; it just can't be splintered like this.

My favorite coffee shop sells an adaptogenic latte that has an undeniable calming effect. I don't know if there's any scientific truth to the claims about the mushrooms in it or if it's simply the power of suggestion, but it works for me. It's unbelievable how much Heath made fun of me for this. Look at him now, hawking products that make far wilder claims. Investing his whole life savings into it. And mine before long. Dammit! Now I'm pissed all over again.

A familiar voice wafts down to me as a hot-bodied shadow falls over my table. "That's decaf, right?"

I put my hands over my cup as if I'm trying to keep the coffee from hearing his words. "Blasphemer." My glare is exaggerated. His grin is sexy as hell, and I don't even care that he's so obviously looking straight down my v-neck. I'm blaming the adaptogens. "What are you doing in my coffee shop?"

"I thought you owned a juice bar."

"I got here first. This place is mine now, too."

"Territorial. I like it." Wick pulls out a chair and joins me. I didn't invite him to sit down. "How's your ass?"

"Off limits." Mentally, I put a few points on my side of the scoreboard because that was a good one.

His eyes go wide like he can't believe I've said it. My spirit of victory ascends to a new level. Then he says, "Damn, how many gauntlets can you throw down in one day?"

"That was not meant to be a challenge."

"But yet." He smirks. "I don't make the rules."

"You just break them."

"Something like that."

"Why are you looking at my latte that way?"

"Just wondering how hot it is. You're unpredictable, and I'm afraid if I say the wrong thing, I might end up with a face full of coffee before I even know what I did wrong."

"Lucky for you, it's been here a while so you won't suffer any permanent disfigurement."

He sticks his finger in it to test it. He. Sticks. His. Finger. In my coffee! Before I can even begin to exhibit my disgust, said finger is in his mouth. *Oof.* He pulls it out and makes a face like he's tasted liquid evil. "What the hell are you drinking?"

"It has mushrooms in it. You get used to it."

"Bold claim."

"Maybe it's your filthy finger that tastes bad."

"Hmm, interesting theory. Maybe I should stick it somewhere else and see how the taste test goes?"

"You can't just talk to women you hardly know like that." *It's not like we routinely carry spare panties around in our purses.*

"I'm not talking to women. I'm talking to one woman. You. And you should get your mind out of the gutter because I meant this." He reaches over and runs the tip of his finger through my cheese Danish. This time he lets it linger in his mouth for a moment, and then he parts his lips so I can see that he's swirling his tongue around it before he sucks it clean. "It's definitely not my finger. That's tasty. Incredibly bad for you, but very, very good."

"Are you describing yourself with that last line, or the Danish?"

"How do you know I'm not talking about you? Although, in my experience, it's hard to make a proper comparison between two things when you've only had one of them. And I've only had the Danish." He stands up, stealing my napkin as he goes. "I should probably let you get back to work." His hand closes to wrench the napkin around his freshly-sucked finger. "Enjoy your bad choices. You'll pay for them at our next session."

"It's cute that you think I'd put up with being disciplined."

He leans down until his mouth is right next to my ear. A rich, woodsy scent fills my nose and I can't help but inhale. "It's cute that you think I'd put up with being disobeyed." His lips brush my ear. I tell myself the contact was accidental, but that doesn't stop me from quivering. "Is it chilly in here?" He sets his big hands on my shoulders and rubs them up and down my arms a few times.

I unintentionally whimper when he takes them away. "Sorry. I didn't mean to make that sound, but my muscles are sore and your hands are warm and . . . " I trail off because continuing to speak right now could only make this more embarrassing.

"Your muscles need heat. I have a hot tub." His hands rest on my shoulders again and he laughs softly at the way I jump under his touch. "Pack up your computer and come with me."

Oh, God. Those words again.

SIX
ADAPTABILITY

The coffee shop is only a few blocks from my place so I always walk over here, which means driving my own car to Wick's place isn't an option. He drives a Jeep Wrangler, and I literally cannot think of a vehicle that would've been less surprising. Of course, he's a Jeep guy. "You travel over a lot of rough terrain?" I ask. "In Houston?"

"I'm not from Houston. I didn't buy it here."

"Oh. That didn't occur to me. Sorry." He holds the passenger side door open for me, which makes me feel like a jerk for teasing him about the Jeep. "Where are you from?" I ask when he slides into the driver's seat.

"Katy."

"Oh, you ass! That's basically part of Houston. You had me feeling all guilty and judgmental, thinking you were from some mountainous state where this thing was actually practical."

"What's practicality got to do with it?" Music blares when he starts the engine. He turns it down and laughs. "Do you know how many times this thing has saved my ass during a flood? Cars were literally filled with water in the gym parking lot last spring because so much rain fell in an hour that people couldn't drive home. They just had to leave their cars there and let them get totaled. Don't tell me it's not a practical vehicle for Houston."

"Okay, I didn't think about flooding. I stand corrected."

"You're adorable when you're humbled. Has anyone every told you that?" He strokes my cheek with the backs of his fingers. It's a touch that feels too tender for a parking lot, and too intimate for someone I barely know.

"Are you kidding? I won that honorific in high school: most adorable when humbled."

"I'd have voted for you." I'm grateful he breaks the moment and puts the car in reverse, but I instantly crave his hand back on my skin.

He lives in one of those newer subdivisions where the houses are so close together you can hear your neighbor spitting out their toothpaste in the morning. Not that I'm going to be doing any spitting while I'm here. Or swallowing. Great. Now my cheeks are flushed at my own thoughts. Why am I like this?

I can sense Wick looking at me. "Everything okay?"

"Yeah, I'm good."

My eyes move over every surface as I follow him into his house. Every hard surface. No carpet. No rugs. No extra pillows on the couch. No curtains on the windows, only blinds. No frills at all. It probably echoes in here.

"I'll grab us some towels."

"Towels?"

"For the hot tub?"

"Um, yeah, I don't have a bathing suit sooo . . ." *So why am I here to begin with?*

"Good news, I wasn't planning on wearing one either." He disappears down a hallway, leaving me standing with my mouth agape.

This guy just says whatever he wants. And I'd be lying if I

said I wasn't already wondering how filthy his mouth is in bed. Or a hot tub.

"Don't worry," he says as he walks back down the hall. "I have privacy screens I can lower around the hot tub so the kids next door can't sneak pictures of you and sell them online."

"Well, I'm totally at ease now."

"Good." He holds a towel out to me. "You probably want to leave your clothes inside so we don't slosh water on them."

"What makes you think there will be sloshing?"

"I keep it pretty full."

"I see."

"You can change in my room. First door on the right."

Am I really going to do this? It's just a body, and I haven't been ashamed of it in years. I'm no more vulnerable naked than in any bathing suit I own. Those few pieces of fabric aren't armor. It's not like I've never taken my clothes off in front of a man the same night I met him, so why am I so hesitant right now?

This is what I secretly hoped would happen when I showed up for the training session today to begin with. Well, not the hot tub, specifically, but definitely being naked together. It's the ultimate revenge, right? Sleep with his friend. Except now I know they're not really friends, and I've never really been the ultimate revenge type to begin with. I'm more the clean break, no looking back type.

Wick is watching me like he's trying to read my thoughts. He probably can. My face speaks out loud far more often than I'd like, usually in the most inopportune moments, so now would be right on cue.

"Hey," he says. "If you're uncomfortable, we don't have to soak. We're cool. We can hang out, watch a movie, order a pizza . . . but it really would help with the soreness. You can sit in the hot tub alone if you want. Whatever. Your call."

No, don't do this. Be the asshole I need you to be so we can get on with the mutually beneficial using and be done. "Please don't be nice to me." My words come out in a thready whisper. "I just need to fuck away the betrayal. And my own stupidity."

"I didn't realize he cheated. I'm sorry."

I don't correct him immediately because the truth of what Heath did feels more hurtful in this moment. It would be easier to say he cheated. But despite my intention not to respond, I do. "He didn't. It's worse."

"Would you like a glass of wine?"

"A big one."

"You got it."

While he's in the kitchen opening the wine, I make a decision about the hot tub. If I'm going to do this, it may as well start in a hot tub with a glass of wine.

When I join him in the kitchen, Wick offers me a glass holding a very generous pour. I reach tentatively, trying to avoid a wardrobe malfunction with my towel in the middle of his kitchen. "Your wine glasses are plastic?" There's no masking the judgment in my question.

"The ones I use in the hot tub are, yes."

"You didn't know I was going to say yes to the hot tub yet."

"Well, I saw you turn and head for the hallway so I figured you were either going to shed your clothes or steal my watch collection. I took my chances."

"I could've been going to the bathroom."

"That probably should've occurred to me as a third option."

"In your mind, I was either getting naked or stealing from you? No other possibility?"

"Full disclosure, I was strongly hoping for naked."

"Are you not taking your clothes off?"

"Am I invited to share the hot tub with you?"

"It's your hot tub."

"It's still your choice."

"Drop your pants." I turn and walk out onto the patio. I'm pretty sure watching him undress might derail the hot tub plans, and my muscles are screaming for some soothing jets and steam.

He walks out with a towel wrapped around his waist, and I swear the only thing that keeps me from yanking it off him is the potential horror of exposing his chiseled nakedness to some innocent young girl, looking out her bedroom window.

I follow him to the raised section of his deck where he refuses my help to remove the cover from the hot tub. "I've got it. Drink your wine."

Once he has the cover off, he turns on the jets and lowers the privacy screens. It's tight quarters, no room for seductively disrobing. He lets his towel hit the deck first, and I swallow a gulp of wine. Once he's submerged in the bubbles, he sets his glass on the side and reaches for mine. Then he reaches for my hand to assist me, but there's just no elegant, or even slightly modest, way to climb into a hot tub. I drop my towel and join him in the water.

This heat feels amazing, but when I climbed in, he slid over to the back left corner, and instead of sliding all the way to the back right, I plopped straight down in the front corner, diagonally across from him, creating the greatest possible distance between us. Moving now would be awkward. So, here we sit with our bodies positioned to ensure no accidental touch, no chance at all of seamlessly moving closer to one another.

The whir of the jets and the rolling water creates a soothing hum-and-whoosh sound. It's still early afternoon, but between the screens and the rising steam, it could be dusk. And we could be anywhere. The perfect escape from reality, and there is nothing I'd rather do than shut out my real life right now.

"Do you want to talk about it?" His steam-kissed skin glistens in the filtered light. This shimmering man, who is hard to look away from, started off so brusque and impersonal that it was easy to volley back-and-forth sarcasm and keep my walls up. But this sincere version of him unnerves me. And no, I don't want to talk about it. I want to resume our flirty banter and forget about it.

Being naked in front of him isn't my biggest concern about being here. Wick might have the power to strip me bare emotionally. Had I seen that coming, I'd still be in the coffee shop, staring at my computer. "It's all related to that supplement company he's into." That's all I offer.

"He's pretty gung-ho about it."

"Yeah. That's putting it mildly. I can't believe he tried to get you to invest in it, too. Forget I said that. I can totally believe it at this point."

"How's the juice bar doing?"

Thank you for the change of subject. "Great."

"You've got an impressive menu. Pricey, but it's good stuff."

"You've been there?"

"Yeah. I hit the drive-through several times a week. I own a juicer but it's a pain in the ass to clean. Totally worth the cost to have someone else do the work." He lifts his wine glass to toast to the convenience.

I lift my glass to return the gesture and I'm stunned to see it's nearly empty. How'd that happen?

He sees what I'm looking at and knows exactly what I'm thinking. "I completely forgot to bring the wine out." Before I can respond to say it's fine, he's rising through the steam and leaning over the edge of the hot tub. As he hoists himself fully over the side, every inch of him comes into view.

And he is indeed sporting many inches. I don't mean to stare but it's all right there. When he catches me surveying him, all his inches respond. My eyes drift to the foam crashing on the surface of the water as if they'd been focused there all along. It's not until he walks away that I realize he'd paused and stood there intentionally, knowing I would check him out. I bite back a smile. *There's that arrogant bastard I need.*

I lean back. Sink down. Relax.

Wick returns with the bottle. And this time, he climbs in at my corner and stays there. He pours us more wine. And then he leans back. Sinks down. Relaxes.

So, here we sit, thigh-to-thigh, his arm around my shoulders, the least possible amount of space between our bodies.

SEVEN
OUT OF MY DEPTH

I shift and my leg slides against his. The slippery friction is a nice feeling, one that leaves me longing, but I'm not making the first move here. I could, but I won't. Okay, I might. But not yet.

"So, what do you do when you're not running a juice bar?"

"Thankfully, we have managers to run it. I couldn't have bought it if I'd had to quit my job. I'm in sales."

"Pharmaceutical?"

"Petrochemical. Shockingly, women are capable of selling things other than anti-depressants, but thanks for the assumption."

"My sister's a pharmaceutical rep. The assumption came from family, not a stereotype. Do you have to go into the refineries?"

"A lot gets done online. I'm only on the road a few days a week. I spend a ridiculous amount of time in meetings and doing paperwork. Sorry for being defensive. Do you work at any other gyms?"

"No, but I have private clients I train at their home gyms

or offices. So many companies have onsite facilities. I just landed my first corporate contract."

"What kind of company offers their employees a personal trainer?"

"People are more productive when they're healthy."

"Still a nice perk."

"Here's to hoping their employees take advantage of it. I'd gladly give up working at the gym and be completely on my own." He smiles at me and adds, "I mean, some days there are good. Every now and then, I meet someone interesting." His thigh presses against mine, teasing me with that skin-on-skin sensation again.

"I'm sure you have no problem meeting women."

"Women are plentiful. Interesting ones? Not so much."

"That is so fucking reductive. Women are *plentiful*? You might as well be talking about rocks."

"Men are plentiful, too. There are a lot of us walking around. But how often do you meet one you want to spend any time with?"

I turn my face toward him. "Not very often."

"See?"

What I see is a perfect pair of lips I can't wait any longer to kiss. His cupid's bow is so symmetrical and defined it looks like it's been painted on. His bottom lip is full and I know it's going to be soft and perfect. I lean in slightly, and that's all the permission he needs.

Sliding his hand up the back of my neck, he pulls me closer, crushing his mouth against mine. There's no gentle kiss that builds in intensity; he goes full throttle and steals my breath from first contact, maintaining a firm grasp on the back of my neck the whole time. His tongue sweeps through my mouth and I liquify.

He pulls me onto his lap, keeping his erection between us. I attempt to lift up, but he denies my effort and forces my hips back down where he'd originally positioned me. He breaks the kiss and pushes against my shoulders to sit me straight up. "Why the rush?" he asks as his gaze skates over my breasts. They've been exposed the whole time we've been out here, but he looks at them now as if he's contemplating a pre-emptive apology.

"I just really need this."

"I don't think you know what you need." He brings his gaze back to my face and there's a new steeliness in his eyes.

"And you do?"

"There's a real good chance." His hands release my hips and roam up my sides. "I think you need to play a little."

"We can play." I rock my hips forward and back and he smiles, but shakes his head, letting me know he has something else in mind.

"What's with the bees?"

I was wondering if he was going to ask about the trio of honeybees looping across my left breast. "I like bees. They're cute."

He clamps my nipples between his thumbs and forefingers. "Very cute." The initial squeezes are gentle but he increases the force, keeping his eyes locked on mine. It's sweet torture— until it becomes less sweet, approaching painful. "Relax, beau- tiful. Close your eyes. Let go."

"Relinquishing control's never been my strong suit."

"You'll learn."

For a split second, I want to object, but I want him more. His whole face has changed, his jaw is tighter, his eyes even more piercing. He pinches harder and I gasp. My spine instinctively tries to retreat but he doesn't let go. "Just breathe. Close your eyes and breathe through it."

I have no reason at all to trust him, but I'm inexplicably inclined to follow his instructions. Closing my eyes challenges my balance. I ignore the pain and focus on breathing normally, suddenly feeling like I'll fall over if I don't concen- trate on holding stone-still right where he wants me. The water is flowing around and between us, pushing and pulling.

Wick starts to roll my nipples, keeping the pressure steady for a few moments before he begins a slow and methodical squeeze and release. I exhale on the first release but when he squeezes again, I suck in so much air I nearly choke. My whole body contracts. "Breathe easy. This is about to feel so good, I promise." On the heels of that reassurance, he pinches harder than before and holds on for what feels like minutes. I can't breathe at all. When he lets go, the rush of endorphins turns my bones to jelly. I rise and fall gently in the water like I'm floating over his lap. My heart's racing but I feel light.

I open my eyes and notice his are lasciviously hooded. The corners of his mouth are upturned ever so slightly. It's almost imperceptible, not quite a smile.

He pulls my body against him, and I collapse on his chest. His hands rub long strokes up and down my back. "When I fuck you, I want nothing else competing for your attention. No stress keeping you tense or drawing your thoughts away from the moment. I want you completely."

His arms scoop and flip me so I'm cradled in his lap. "Let your legs fall open." I hesitate and his voice takes on a sterner timbre. "Open your legs." They fall apart and my head lolls on his shoulder. "There you go. That's a good girl." He fingers me under the water and we both laugh softly when he says, "You are so wet." It's such a juvenile joke but laughing relaxes me a bit more. The combination of the heat and the wine has my nerve endings all simmering, but I know he could bring me to a rolling boil at will. And sweet Jesus, do I hope he will soon.

His thumb teases around my clit and I practically nuzzle into the crook of his neck. Mmmmm, yeah, this is nice. I'm perfectly okay with staying here for a while, splayed open on his lap like a sedated cat. He chooses this exact moment of contented bliss to make a direct assault on my clit. My hips jerk and my receptors all blink back on at full power.

His low villainous laugh only makes me want him more. As soon as I settle under the direct pressure on my clit, he backs off, resumes circling the periphery. I shift my pelvis to chase his thumb and he laughs again. "What do you want?"

"Make me come."

"Do you mean *let* you come?"

"Uh-huh."

"What?"

"Yes."

"Yes what?"

"Yes, please."

"No, I'm not asking you to beg. Yes, who?"

I flutter my eyes open and glare at him through my lashes. But fuck me, he's hot and he's good and if I have to give him what he wants to get what I want, fine. "Yes, sir." *My pussy did not just clench at that. Traitorous cunt. Literally.*

His smile pulls his jaw tighter. "Such a good girl."

He withdraws his fingers from my pussy. I instantly want him to reinsert them, but then he scissors them at the sides of my clit, kneading and swiping across it with every crisscrossing maneuver. No one has ever done this to me before, and it's not something I could do to myself, not like this, anyway. His fingers are wide. They cover more area than mine ever could. It's a sensation I simultaneously want to escape and intensify. But it's not one I'm going to be able to relax into. No, this is going to keep me on the razor's edge until I shatter.

My teeth capture my bottom lip and I will myself with every fiber in my body to be still and breathe evenly. But nothing short of falling into a spontaneous coma could keep my ass from trembling as my clit swells between his fingers. My legs start to shake next, and there's no way my hips are staying level for another minute.

I suck in rapid tiny breaths until they become longer

inhales with no chance to exhale in between, and then gasps, bordering on shrieks, until a hard jolt that I can only describe as a pleasurable electrocution zaps my clit, sending shock-waves into my core that zing out through my limbs until even the tips of my fingers and toes are tingling with alternating currents of ecstasy and agony. If I die, I die.

The neighbors may not have been able to see anything through these privacy screens, but I sure hope their windows were closed as well, because I made some sounds. I just . . . I made *some sounds*. And now I'm not sure I can even speak. I hope he plans to stay in control, because my body's ability to top just bottomed the fuck out.

He kisses my forehead and strokes my cheek with the backs of his fingers again. "When was the last time you were bent over the edge of a hot tub?"

"Years ago."

"I'm about to make that memory pale in comparison. Get on your knees, beautiful." He slides me off his lap onto the bench seat.

With my back to him, I go up onto my knees and grip the edge for a moment before I slide down, bring my forearms to rest on the side, and push my hips back and up. He knees my legs farther apart, and then steps back. A shiver of anticipa-tion ripples up my spine. Moments pass without him moving closer or touching me. He leaves me in his requested position to wonder how much longer . . . when will the promised memory paling begin? Somehow, I know if I look over my shoulder or question him, he'll prolong it more.

A siren wails in the distance. I listen while it gets louder and louder as it races closer and closer, and then fades as it drives on toward the emergency. My own breathing adopts the pattern of the siren, quickening with the increased volume, and now steadying as it trails off, confirming there's no imme-diate threat. Fight or flight deactivated. Nothing to fear.

Wick finally steps closer, his erection pressing against my

ass for a few seconds before he secures his footing. His knuckles fleetingly brush my tender skin when he brings his dick to my pussy. Phantom strokes persist on my cheek, reminding me of his earlier shows of compassion.

The swollen head of his cock pressing at my opening ratchets up my anticipation. He advances slowly, stretching me inch-by-inch, and I don't know how he has the restraint to keep from slamming his full length to the hilt but that's what I want. *Just fuck me already.*

I rock my hips back to urge him deeper, and he halts completely. I don't need to look back to know he's smiling. When he moves again, it's with one firm, fluid stroke that takes him balls-deep and fills me completely.

My walls clench around him, and this is a sensation I'd like to savor for a while. We're apparently on the same page now. With my eyes closed, I stitch this moment into my memories, gathering the smell of the chlorine, the heaviness of the steam in the air, his fingers gripping my hips, the unforgiving plastic under my knees, the tickle of droplets as they break free and trickle down my neck . . .

His voice wends its way into the vignette—a low, lurid rasp. "You like having your sweet little snatch full of cock, don't you?"

"Yes."

He begins to withdraw and I intentionally squeeze to try to hold him in, but he keeps going until only the head remains inside me. With no pause, he glides back in, picking up speed, but not nearly enough to satisfy my yearning. His fingers dig into my flesh and he says, "I need your safe word."

My brain spins out. I never even had a safe word until two years ago, and that word was only for him. With Heath, I used the stoplight system: red, yellow, green. Honestly, I can't imagine using a safe word with Wick right now, but I probably shouldn't take anything for granted when it comes to him.

"Scale," I blurt.

"Scale is your safe word?"

I look over my shoulder. "It is with you."

His grin spreads slowly. "I get an exclusive word? I'm flattered."

"Make me use it."

He said he never met a challenge he didn't want to take. I hope he's ready to back up that claim because I'm definitely ready to experience his A game.

"How about a friendly wager?" he proposes. "If I can make you use your safe word, I win. If not, you win."

"What's the prize?"

"Let's keep it interesting. Winner gets to choose. Loser can't refuse."

EIGHT
LET THE GAMES BEGIN

I face forward again, and prepare to be railed into submission. I'm fully braced for it, but I'm not at all prepared for him to maintain this leisurely pace as if I haven't just thrown the gauntlet. As if winner's choice isn't on the line. Why won't he go for it?

Ohhhhh, I get it. He's going to try to keep it so vanilla I can't take it anymore, try to bore me to my breaking point. He likes games. Never going to happen. *Give it your all, big guy. Or your least. Whatever. I got nowhere else to be.*

It's not like what he's doing right now doesn't feel good. He's got a nice dick, and even though he's refusing to show me just how well he can use it, this isn't terrible. I'll give him a little while before I turn the tables on him.

I bring one hand on top of the other to make a pillow, and then I lay my head down and watch the shadows of tree limbs dancing across the privacy screen. He keeps his rhythm steady. I close my eyes and smile. Damn, if I'm not careful, I could be lulled to sleep in no time at all. I didn't get much sleep last night and I didn't really eat much today – half a Danish before somebody stuck his finger in it. I'm already feeling wine-headed. I could honestly doze off way too easily, so I go ahead and start toying with him now.

First, I let out a slow, salacious moan, not entirely sure I can pull it off without laughing. But I think it sounds believable enough. I desperately wish I could see his face but there's no way I'm opening my eyes. "I guess you were right about me not knowing what I wanted. This is incredible." I moan again, and rock my hips back to meet his next lazy thrust. "Please don't change anything. Oh, God, yes. I'm going to come if you keep doing it just like this."

"I promise, sweetheart. I won't change a thing."

Well, fuck. That didn't go like I'd planned. I guess I'm not the only one good at reading people. Pretty sure he knows exactly what I'm doing. But it still comes down to a battle of wills and that's not a game I lose. I prolong my next moan, rolling my head and shoulders as if I've been possessed by passion.

"This is so pleasant," he says. "I really like seeing how much you enjoy my lovemaking." Seriously? I know his mouth can get filthy. He's already shown that card. But that's fine. I can take his cringy words. I didn't fall for reverse psychology as a kid; it's sure not going to work on me now. "Is this the best you've ever had?" he asks.

"Yes, sir." I practically mewl the words. "Your thick, hard cock feels so good. I've never been stretched like this before." Oh, that dick jumped. I felt it. "Please keep giving it to me just like this." I make sure my voice is breathy, and I exploit the gift of the Kegels as I plead for more of this sweet, sweet remedial intercourse. *Here we go. We've got increased swelling. Give me that pre-detonation pulse and I will take you down.*

He rubs my ass, his wide palm covering an entire cheek. *Slap it. Shit. I can't say it out loud, but thinking it doesn't end my performance. I'm in it to win it.* His hand coasts all the way up my back until he can reach my ponytail. He gingerly twirls it. *Pull it.*

Come on. Just one hard tug? When he releases my hair, a few strands catch on his fingers and there's a tense twinge at my scalp. Was that really an accident? From this position, there's no way I can retaliate with an accidental touch of my own.

I'm trying to think of what I can say next when his fingers slide between my legs. Oh. Is he switching tactics? Not that I'm objecting.

But, no. He doesn't get anywhere near my clit, just rubs hard circles on my labia, which might be the most goddamn annoying thing I've ever felt. Until he starts kneading it like Play-Do. It's fine. All I have to do is think of something that can transport me away from this basic pedestrian penetration while his hand tries to turn my vulva into a pinch pot. I could learn to hate this guy. I already wanted to hate-fuck him, but up to this point, the anger behind it has been about Heath, not him.

Oh, he's good. He wants me to direct all that feral energy toward him, not some other guy. Wants me completely, just like he said. Great! Not like I can hate him now, but I really hate having my pussy kneaded like modeling clay. Fuck it. "Scale."

"Nooooo," he says. "Come on. I had so many more bad moves planned."

I laugh. "If you're going to leave me sore, I'd prefer it at least be internal."

"Okay, okay." He laughs, too. "Relax. No more teasing, I promise." I'm not sure if he's serious or he's setting me up here, but I lean forward and rest my head on my hands again.

Within seconds, I know he is serious. He lessens the space between us and kisses my neck. His warm breath ghosts over my ear as he whispers, "I'm definitely going to leave you sore, but first, I'm going to make you come on my hand."

"Don't you mean *let* me come on your hand?"

"Exactly." He bites down playfully at the base of my neck.

"Can you do that again, but harder?" His teeth sink

deeper this time and my pussy juices. We're definitely done playing games with each other.

"I like that you're not afraid to ask for what you want." He continues kissing and biting my neck and shoulders, and his fingers expertly work my clit. I come undone for him in a matter of minutes, and between the orgasm and the heat, I'm spent. But I know we're not finished.

His fingers slip away from my still throbbing clit and his hands take hold of my hips. I inhale, knowing he's about to fuck me right.

He does it so very right. My ribcage scrapes over the side of the hot tub with every forceful thrust. Tomorrow, my whole torso might be bruised and battered, but right now, this is exactly what I want. He pulls my ponytail to bring my head back so he can bite my neck again, and I moan for real.

"Is this hard enough for you?" he asks in a husky whisper.

"Yes. But if you need more, I can take it."

"Don't say that." He drives into me with extra force this time.

"Why not?"

"Because I might believe you."

"I wouldn't make the offer if I didn't mean it."

He groans, and it leaves raw, growly undertones lingering in my ears. His hand moves away from my hair again and wraps over the top of my shoulder. With his other hand still securely grasping my hip, he holds me in place and rams his granite-hard cock into me. The water carries me forward every time, and if he didn't have such a firm hold on my shoulder and hip, I'd fear being launched over the side. He tightens his grip on me and it hurts, but in the best way possible.

My original intention was to be a more active participant when we reached this point, but being used like this is better. I need him to keep using me until he's done because tomorrow, when the fucking is long over, the low-level aches and soreness in my body will be a counterweight for the emotional pain of everything else happening in my life. Not a perfect balance, but better than nothing.

Wick's release erupts with barbaric sounds and thrusts, and his grip becomes a crushing vise when the spasticity seizes his body at the height of his pleasure.

His muscles relax as the jets of the hot tub cycle back on. I breathe in lungsful of steam and feel like I'm exactly where I'm meant to be right now, as if this whole encounter were pre-destined. My body is a heap of exhaustion. I look down at our soaked towels. Suffice to say, there was sloshing.

He kisses my neck, and I smile. "I want to take you inside and hold you hostage in my bed until morning."

"Do you promise to leave your handprint on my ass if I agree?"

"Are you trying to get me to give you a key?"

"No. Just a little more manhandling. And maybe a few more glasses of wine."

"How about dinner first?"

"You'll have to have it delivered. I don't think I could walk all the way from the car into a restaurant."

"Now you're just trying to get me to carry you inside the house."

"I think I can manage that many steps. But it's going to be a slippery journey." I turn and smile at him. "Our towels are drenched."

"Guess the neighbors are getting a show after all."

"A gentleman would offer to go in and bring me back a dry towel."

"I can be a gentleman. But don't you dare start acting like a lady."

He climbs out and cranks the lever that raises the privacy screen, halting it a few feet above the edge of the hot tub. I watch as he ducks under, stands tall on the other side, and walks away, leaving wet footprints on the deck.

If there is indeed a young girl watching him, seeing her first naked man, I'm no longer worried about her being corrupted by it. The real travesty would be the way it would set her up for so much future disappointment.

NINE
STRIKING OUT

After we've dried off fully in his bedroom, Wick tosses me one of his t-shirts. I catch it but give him a quizzical look. He shrugs. "If you prefer to sleep naked, you won't get any complaints from me."

"I never said I was sleeping here." There's no way I'm staying. But this t-shirt is soft and my body is still warm from the hot tub. Seems like a more comfortable option. I can't help but smile at him before I pull his shirt over my head. For such a cocky guy, he's awfully nice. Too nice.

He scoffs when I step into my underwear. "You really feel like you need those."

"There might be a fire."

"They're flame-proof?"

I laugh. It's not fair for a guy to look like he does and have such a quick wit, too. He should have to wear a warning sign. "I hope I never have to find out. But just in case."

"What do you want on your pizza? Please don't say pineapple."

"You can get toppings on just one half, you know."

"Not pineapple. It ruins the whole thing."

"You've probably never even tried it."

"I don't have to try it to know I won't like it." He taps his phone screen. "I know you like mushrooms."

The comment startles me. How would he know that? Oh, yeah. He's talking about my latte. That he stuck his finger in. This whole encounter happened because he stuck his finger in my coffee. And my Danish. And his mouth. "Yeah, I like mushrooms. And olives. Green though, not the black ones."

He sticks out his tongue and scrunches his face up like he's tasted poison. Or my latte. "Hard no. Mushroom and pepperoni."

"No pepperoni. Sausage."

"Deal."

We are never going to agree on a movie. "You promised me more wine."

"I said you should eat first."

"I compromised on the pizza. I deserve a glass of wine now."

"You are going to be begging for mercy at tomorrow's workout."

"I don't work out with you again until Friday."

"No, you're on my books for seven a.m. tomorrow. Trust me." His sexy smile makes me rethink staying the night, but if we're really working out in the morning, I definitely have to go home. I'm not a gym rat. There's not a bag of emergency workout clothes in my car. It's okay that he put me on his schedule without asking me first though. It might be the only thing that makes me go home tonight. The last thing I need is to wake up to a walk of shame. I'm carrying enough shame right now to last me. Wick tugs my ponytail as he walks past. "Okay, wino. Come with me."

Sir, you have got to quit saying those words.

I was right about our inability to agree on a movie, but he likes true crime shows so it works out. Okay, he may have said he likes police procedurals and I may have bargained for true crime instead. Whatever. I was probably going to suck his dick later anyway. Let him think he really won one.

For the second morning in a row, I want to smash my phone when the alarm goes off. But, wait. That's not my alarm sound. I open one eye. *Oh, shit. I stayed. It's all coming back to me now. Walk of shame, coming in hot.* Wick rolls to reach his phone and my head throbs. Yeah, there is no way I'm working out this morning.

"Rise and shine," he says. His voice is raspy and the phrase sounds more sarcastic than motivated.

"I can't do either one of those things right now."

"Thank fuck." He rolls toward me and half-grins as his eyelids close.

I should get up and go home but it hurts to open my eyes, and driving home with my eyes closed would be a terrible idea . . . oh, damn. I walked to the coffee shop. What the hell was I thinking, letting him drive us over here instead of making him take me to my car so I could follow him? I open my eyes to look at him again. His eyes are still closed but he shakes his head as if he can feel me looking at him, and says, "Ssshhhhh. Sleep."

Pretty sure I've done everything else he's commanded. Why stop now?

When we wake again, it's nearly nine and we're in agreement that we have to get up and get going this time. "Want a smoothie? I know a great place," he says as I reluctantly put my clothes back on. "That Magic Elixir juice shot is as close to a hangover cure as anything I've ever tried. And we both need hydration."

"I cannot go to my own juice bar looking like this." My

ponytail has fallen lower but it's still in the hair tie. It flops over my shoulder when I lean forward to pull up my pants, and the smell of my chlorinated hair makes me wretch.

"I'll park and go inside to get them. Won't even make you cower in the drive-through. Because I'm a nice guy like that." He sets a ballcap on my head when I stand upright again. "But you can borrow this as an added precaution."

"Thanks." I pull it down onto my head, and then I instinctively use both hands to bend the bill inward the way I like it.

"Did you seriously just do that to my hat?"

"It was an accident. You can flatten it back out."

He sighs. "It's fine. Not like it was a commemorative Astros World Series cap or anything."

"Right. I forgot you're on the team." I roll not just my eyes, but my whole head. "Why do fans deserve to wear World Series caps? It's not like you knocked in the winning run or anything."

"Are you always this mean in the mornings?"

"No. I'm sorry. I'll buy you another hat. I promise." I ache. I stink. I want to cry and punch something at the same time. Repeatedly. I thought yesterday morning was going to be the hardest, but this one hurts in new ways. My mind is racing with all things I have to make right somehow, and it's too much. I don't know how I'm supposed to keep getting out of bed and pushing through this shit day after day. I'm sorry I messed up his precious fucking hat but give me a break. It's just a hat.

"Don't worry about it. It's fine." His voice is monotone.

I turn to follow him out of his bedroom and see the frames taking up valuable book space on his shelves. Team photos. A news release? I step closer to read it. *Fuuuuck me.* "You played professional baseball?"

"Just minor league. Made it to triple A, but that was it. Not like I won the World Series or anything." He flips out the light and walks off down the hall.

I can honestly say that's the first time I've ever shit on someone's broken dreams. He's right. I am mean. There's no juice shot for what I'm going through. *Who do I talk to about opting out of my villain era? Because thanks, I hate it!*

TEN
WE'LL SEE

You'd think a CPA would be punctual but Paula is already ten minutes late for our meeting. I'd have been on time if we'd met at her office, but it was her idea to meet for lunch instead, and I apparently don't deserve the same courtesy. I'm not even hungry since Wick still insisted that we get smoothies this morning, even after I was a jerk. I stir my iced tea but there's no sweetener in it. I'm just fidgety.

Wick was kind again when he dropped me off at my place, which only made me madder at myself. I don't see me showing up for another training session. Would it really be too much to ask for a guy to want to hit and quit it like the good old days? Noooo, he wants to grab dinner this weekend, maybe go somewhere afterwards for a few drinks, get to know each other better. Who asked him to be decent? Nobody!

"Hi, sorry I'm late." Paula hangs her purse on the back of the chair before she sits down. "There was a tanker on its side across I-10, spilling who knows what all over the road. My whole car is probably covered in carcinogens now." She gives me a half-smile. "Sorry. I know that's your industry but, damn. You'd think they could be a little more responsible."

"I have nothing to do with trucks or drivers or any other mode of transport. That's all above my paygrade."

"You forget I've seen your paygrade." She laughs now. "I know it's not your fault I had to drive through an invisible cloud of poison. You have enough problems on your plate without me laying that one on you."

"Thanks."

We keep it simple and both order the same lunch special. As soon as the server walks away, Paula looks across the table at me and says, "So, I have some interesting news."

"You'd like to offer me a chance to get in on the ground floor of an exclusive investment opportunity?"

"No, smartass. But I do love your dark sense of humor. Hold on to that." She squeezes a lemon wedge over her water glass. "The other Skweez franchisee in Houston is very interested in your store. I reached out on a lark, just to take his temperature." She shrugs. "There was a gap in my schedule. Anyway, turns out he's ready to add a second location, and he's very envious of yours."

"What made you think that was a good idea?"

"We just had a brief conversation. I didn't make any promises. If you want to pursue it, you'd need to do it through your attorney, of course. There's no guarantee corporate would approve it, but there's no logical reason why they shouldn't. His store is over two years old and thriving."

"My store's thriving, too."

"Sure, aside from the fact that you just had to make a capital contribution to meet payroll. You know you need to pursue legal action against Heath, right?"

I feel sick. "Wow. Your professional opinion is that I should try to sell." That hurts, feels like she doesn't think I have what it takes to come back from this. Like she's underestimating me.

"And pursue legal action against Heath."

"How much did you tell the owner of the other store?"

"Only that I'm your CPA. I made it out like I was cold

calling him to offer my services. He has no idea you might be willing to sell."

"That makes two of us because I have no idea about that either." The server sets our plates between us but we don't look up at him. We're locked in a stare and I'm trying to decide if I'm angry at Paula or grateful. She overstepped, there's no doubt. But this is useful information.

"Just keep it in your back pocket as an option."

My phone lights up with an incoming text.

Oakley: *How was your training session? I meant to call you last night but Garth got sick and I had to fill in at an event at the last minute. Are you sore today?*

Me: *I wouldn't have been available to take your call. Session ran long. Very long. Very thick. Very, very sore.*

Oakley: *Nade . . .*

Me: *Oak . . .*

Oakley: *I'm cooking tonight. Come eat with us.*

Me: *I'd be more tempted if Hollis was cooking.*

Oakley: *Seven o'clock.*

Me: *We'll see.*

She doesn't respond. She knows I'll show up.

Paula picks up the tab for lunch and I let her—not because I can't afford it, but I'm still not sure if I'm mad at her or not, and I feel like maybe she owes me at least lunch for meddling in my business like that. And being late.

I have more than enough leftovers from lunch to cover dinner, but I put the box in the fridge and tell myself it'll be just as good for lunch tomorrow. I'm definitely having dinner at Oakley's. I'd be a fool not to go. Hollis buys the good wine.

Work phone calls consume my whole afternoon, but I'm always at my best when I'm being productive. I check tasks off my to-do list and make new appointments for next week. This feels good. Normal. I go to the kitchen to refill my water bottle, and my eyes land on my Skweez cup still on the counter where I left it, waiting to be rinsed and tossed in the recycling bin. The stupid smiling lemon on the logo has me smiling back at it. It's not an overly creative design, borderline clichéd even, but it's cute. Memorable. And that's all it needs to be. People are drawn back to images they can't forget, even when it's an unconscious memory.

I sit in my car for a few minutes, staring at the big house with its well-lit winding sidewalk. Oakley loved his old house but Hollis was determined to build a new one when he asked her to move in, one they could design together. This one has her signature all over it, from the huge front porch to the balconies off nearly every room on the second floor. She has a thing for balconies. I make my way to the bright blue front door and press the copper dragonfly doorbell. Hollis answers wearing navy sweats and a faded Texans t-shirt that looks like he's probably owned it since he played for them, and he's been retired from the NFL since I was in college, maybe longer.

"I hope you didn't get all dressed up for dinner on my account," I tease. I'm wearing baggy red jogging shorts and a black Buc-ee's tank, so it's not like I dressed to impress tonight. *Beaver in a ballcap, table for one.* I hold my top away from my body and look down at the silly mascot for the only place I know of where you can fill your tank at one of the eleventy-seven gas pumps (all of which will probably be occupied), grab a fifty-two-ounce cup of coffee, a cinnamon roll the size of your face, a three-pound bag of jerky, a hammock, and some fuzzy pajamas (also bearing the beaver in a ballcap logo). Basically, it's the store you want to be trapped in when the apocalypse hits. "We are both dressed like total Houston stereotypes," I say, letting the material of my shirt fall back into place.

"Two of the best shirts in town." He holds the door wide

to welcome me inside. "But I thought it impressed women when we wore sweats."

"Don't flirt with me. I'm weak." We both laugh. "Anyway, those are the wrong kind. We like the gray ones. Light gray."

"Now you tell me." He throws his arms up. "Oakley's in the kitchen. You want a glass of wine?"

"When have I ever turned down wine in this house?" I drop my purse on a side table as I follow the scent of garlic and basil through the living room and into the kitchen, where I find Oakley leaning over a pot at the exact moment the sauce burps and a hot spatter of marinara hits her cheek.

"Jesus fuck!" she yells as she pulls her face back and swipes her hand over the sauce assault.

"Stir it and turn down the heat, Rachel Ray. I can't believe you're making homemade sauce."

"Enjoy it. I'm going back to the jar after tonight. I knew making it from scratch was overrated."

"Did you cut yourself?" Hollis shouts as he walks back down the hall from the wine cellar. *The wine cellar—it still blows my mind that my best friend lives in a house like this.*

"Do you always have to assume I've cut myself just because I'm in the kitchen?" she shouts back at him.

"To be fair," I say, "you are a menace with a sharp knife."

Hollis sets the bottle on the counter and moves toward Oakley with panicked steps. "You cut your face?"

I laugh at his overreaction. "That's not blood. It's dinner."

"Oh." He pulls her face toward him so he can get a closer look, and then he licks her cheek. "Mmmm, way better than the stuff in a jar."

Oakley wipes her face and giggles, and I gag. "Gross. Could I get that wine now, please?"

Helping Oakley finish up dinner in her gourmet kitchen is a better alternative than eating leftovers alone in my outdated duplex, feeling sorry for myself. *This was supposed to be the year I bought my own place. Now I have to choose between that and saving my business.* I bring a knife down on a stack of romaine leaves like I'm hacking my way through the jungle with a machete.

Oakley glances over her shoulder. "Whoa. What'd that lettuce ever do to you? I guess it's safe to say to say you didn't get all your frustration worked out at the gym."

"I might get another chance tomorrow morning."

"Maybe he'll work you harder next time." She raises her eyebrows and waits for me to share about my time with Wick, but I just smile, and finish prepping the salad in a more civilized manner. We both know she'll get details later.

After dinner, Hollis excuses himself, says he has some emails he needs to follow up on. He always does this when he knows one of us is having a hard time—makes some excuse about work, and then makes himself scarce to give me and Oakley time alone to talk. "I guess you've filled him in," I say.

"Just hit him with the highlights. Are you okay?"

"No. I'm really not. I've got therapy Monday morning. I just saw her two weeks ago and everything was great. I mentioned I was starting to worry about Heath's growing obsession with Bounty of the Seas, but that was the worst of my problems. Hope she has plenty of coffee before I show up." I laugh at the absurdity of the disparity between then and now. "I loaded my schedule with sales calls and meetings for next week."

"Staying busy is good."

"Paula thinks I should try to sell the juice bar."

"Might not be a bad idea."

"It feels too soon to jump ship. She also thinks I should take legal action against Heath but I want to at least give him a chance to repay the money first."

"For how long? Has he indicated he can get the money back?"

I down the last of my wine. "Nope. But maybe he can take out a personal loan or something. I don't know."

"Oh, yeah, he seems like a great credit risk." She takes a

sip of her wine, and sighs when she sets her glass back on the table. "I'm sorry. I promised myself I wouldn't say unhelpful things about him until this was all settled and I knew you were okay."

"You promised me that, too."

"Well, clearly, I'm not capable and I need to rage about him already because he fucking stole from you, Nade!"

"He's on the account though. We're partners. This is a whole mess. Yes, I could call an attorney and involve corporate, but if I'm in a legal battle with my partner, it just seems like that would make everything harder. The guy who owns the other Skweez franchise in Houston might want to buy our store. I'm not ready to explore that yet, but it's probably best if there's no ongoing litigation in case it comes to that. Don't you think?"

"I think you need professional legal advice. Hollis thinks so, too. Call Marlise, please. She handled the deal for you when you bought in. Who better to help you now? Please, please protect yourself, Nade. I'm worried, okay?"

"I'm scared shitless, Oakley. I just don't understand how everything could go so wrong so fast. I guess it couldn't hurt to hear what Marlise thinks." I know she's brilliant. The truth is, I'm embarrassed to tell her this has happened. Her clients are all billionaires. She only worked with me in the first place because Hollis sent me her way. But she represents a lot of professional athletes, so it's not like she's never had a client get burned by their own bad decisions before. And if there's anything I need right now, it's probably a brilliant, badass attorney in my corner.

"Brace yourself. She doesn't mince words."

"I know. That's exactly why I'm considering it."

"Good. Did I tell you I'm planning a party for Hollis's fortieth birthday?"

"I thought he said no to a party, and y'all were taking a trip instead."

"Technically, he just said he'd *rather* go on a trip. He booked a trip and I'm planning him a surprise party, so he gets both."

"And he just loves when you creatively interpret what he says."

"He's the king of creative interpretation. And he loves parties. It's going to be great."

Most people prefer to leave their jobs at the office, but Oakley's an event planner and it's her favorite personal pastime as well.

She puts a full bottle of wine in my hands before I leave. "Here. We just bought a whole case of this. You'll like it."

"The dinner guest is supposed to bring a bottle of wine, not leave with one."

"You're not a guest, you're family. Merry Christmas."

"It's July."

"You never heard of Christmas in July?"

"Thanks for dinner. And the wine."

"Call Marlise." She watches me drive away, waving at my car like I'm headed off on a cross-country trip. How someone raised by the coldest mom in coldtown turned out to be one of the warmest, most caring people on the planet, I'll never know.

When I crawl into bed, I send Marlise an email to set up an appointment. I have her cell number but this feels like a time to be as formal as possible. Before I put my phone on the charger, a text comes in.

Wick: *See you in the morning. 7:00 a.m.*

Me: *I'll bring your hat back.*

Wick: *That's your hat now. Don't be late. Eat a light breakfast. No caffeine.*

Me: *I can't be anywhere that early on no caffeine.*

Wick: *I'll buy you coffee after we're done. Real coffee.*

Wick: *But you'll work for it. Trust me.*

Me: *We'll see how I feel in the morning.*

Wick: *See you at seven.*

So sure of himself. I set an alarm. We'll see.

I close my eyes and immediately see his smiling face through the steam rising from his hot tub. When I roll onto my back, the image shifts to his finger entering my latte and then his mouth. My own fingers slide between my legs, and more images of him scroll behind my eyelids.

ELEVEN
PERSONAL DAY

I t will never stop amazing me how many people come to the gym this early. Wick's eyebrows lift when I walk through the door. He can't really be that surprised to see me. "You're late," he says. "Lucky for you, I don't have anyone coming in right behind you. I'll extend your time to make sure you get the full hour."

Hooray! "What if that doesn't work for my schedule? Maybe I have somewhere more important to be and can't stay longer."

"You show up late *and* full of sass?" He comes around the counter and smiles. "No worries. I'll work that out of you." A male voice laughs behind me—that *nice one, bro* kind of a laugh, and if Wick's deep tone hadn't already rendered me a little weak-kneed, I'd spin around and tell whoever finds him so funny to fuck off. "I'm leaving here at 8:30." I head toward the locker room. "I'll be ready in five."

"I'm adding that five to your session, too!" he yells after me.

I bite back the smile trying to form on my flushed face. Challenging people, igniting their inner competitive spirit, is probably a tactic he uses with all his clients, but damn, he turns mine into a raging inferno. I had to circle the parking lot twice looking for a decent spot, and I considered going back home the whole time. Now, I'm ready to sweat.

"Go lower," Wick says, judging my squat technique, and apparently deciding I'm not giving it my all. "Just a few more inches for your last three. You can do it."

My quads are screaming and my glutes are locking up but I force myself to sit down a little lower to finish out the set. It's the last one and all I want to do is break form, relax, and stand up straight—or hit the floor. The face I'm making can't be pretty and I'm shaky as hell, but I exhale and force my muscles to lift me, slow and controlled.

"That's my girl!"

His girl? Relax. It's just an expression. Move your legs before they fuse in place. I lift one leg and shake it out, then the other. My spine pops when I put my hands on my hips and do a partial backbend.

"Grab your ankles."

"Excuse me?"

His eyes meet mine. My own stay wide but his narrow. The only thing wide on his face is his smile. "To release your lower back. You can just fold forward and rag-doll instead if you prefer."

"I do yoga." It's been a while, but whatever. "I know how to release my lower back."

"Well, now would be a good time for it. You'll thank me later."

"I'll thank myself later." I can't do it. I cannot bend over for him right now. My muscles want to, but my brain won't allow it. The last time I gave in and followed his commands after my workout, I woke up in his bed the next morning. I know stretching is technically still part of a workout, but I'll be fine. "I'm going to grab a shower and get going."

"You're not leaving here without stretching."

"What are you going to do, force me to bend over?"

He steps closer and lowers his voice to a coarse whisper. "We can do some partner stretching if you'd rather get on the floor and spread your legs for me."

Now it's my eyebrows reaching for the rafters. *No boundaries. None.* Wick nods his head to another client and trainer sitting on the floor a few yards away from us, legs spread and soles of their shoes touching. The trainer holds her wrists and pulls her forward to assist her stretching. *Oh. That's what he meant. He made it sound dirty on purpose though. It's wasn't just in my head.*

I fold forward and let my head hang heavy. If it could, my lower back would sigh as my spine stretches. This does feel good. I grab my elbows with opposite hands and rock side to side before I stand up. Wick is holding a foam roller out to me. "Roll out those quads. Do you know how to use it?"

"Yes. You do remember whose training session I'm using here, right?"

"Right." He coughs and I can tell he's holding back words. "Some power lifters don't always take stretching as seriously as they should. In my experience, anyway."

"You're not wrong, but I know how to use it." I take the roller from him and drop to the floor, draw in a deep breath to psyche myself up for the pain of torturing my quads on this hard foam. Oh, damn. This hurts so good—the kind of pain you have to laugh through even though there's nothing funny about it.

Wick stands over me, also laughing, but he for sure finds my pain humorous. All those squats after the excessive amount of leg work that he'd already made me do was uncalled for. Who ends a workout with squats? Sadists, that's who. At least he took it easy on my upper body today. On second thought, my shoulders and back suffered plenty, and my triceps are starting to feel like they may have been unwitting accomplices.

When I stop and announce I can't take any more time on the roller, Wick offers me a hand up with a little too much force. I stumble forward, nearly crashing into him. He totally did that on purpose but he acts shocked. "Whoa. Easy. You okay?"

I smirk at him. "Smartass." His hand holds onto mine a few seconds too long to be professional. And if he could stop shooting sparks through my body, that would be great. "I-I need to hit the shower."

"Busy day ahead?"

"Yeah." *Liar.* I'm going home to fall face-first into my bed. The only reason I decided to show up here this morning was to hopefully exhaust my body to the point I can sleep. Last night was another long one with my brain refusing to shut off, even after a few glasses of the wine Oakley sent me home with. I should probably drink some water on the way back to the locker room.

I could wait and shower at home but I'd take my time in my own shower and that's my best thinking spot and there's no way my thoughts wouldn't start cartwheeling again . . . if I thought I could sleep with no shower at all, I'd skip it altogether.

"I was going to offer you another hot tub session, but I guess if you're booked . . ."

Not falling for that again. "Raincheck?" *No, don't encourage him. What the hell?*

"You got it. Make sure you drink a lot of water today."

"Will do. See you Monday, I guess."

"Ouch. Way to shut me down for the weekend."

I laugh, shake my head, and turn to walk away from him. "I'm sure you'll have no trouble filling your weekend."

"We've already had this conversation." I keep walking but he has more to say. "Someday, you're going to let me take you on an actual date instead of just using me for my hot tub." One of the other trainers looks up from wiping down a machine and shoots a knowing glance between me and Wick.

I call over my shoulder, "And someday, maybe you'll learn to whisper things that shouldn't be shouted."

Wick catches up to me, matches my stride, leans in, and proves his ability to whisper. "You and I both know that when the words are dirty and meant for your ears only, I can whisper you wet." A shiver rolls across my shoulders and I can't even try to hide it. "I'm going to call you tomorrow and ask for more of your time."

"And I'm going to politely decline," I whisper back.

"No, you're going to be incredibly sore and ready to cash in that raincheck. You may as well bring a nice change of clothes with you so I can take you to dinner after we're done in the hot tub."

He turns and jogs back down the hall, leaving me at a loss for words. And undeniably wet. Presumptuous bastard. Gorgeous, gorgeous presumptuous bastard.

Taking a personal day on a Friday is always a good idea, but today, it feels especially needed. I'll spend the next few days catching up on rest before I burn up the roads with sales calls next week. Working out this morning was all I'm doing today.

I change out of my shorts and Buffalo Bayou Brewing Co. tee into a much thinner, softer t-shirt before I crawl into my bed. The soft cotton reminds me of sleeping in Wick's shirt. Great! Now I'm never going to get any sleep.

My phone buzzes with an incoming text. It's like radar has alerted him that the feeling of thin cotton brushing across my nipples made me think of him.

But it's not Wick.

It's Heath. Oh, well. Who needed a nap, anyway?

Heath: *Hey, all the money is going to be put back into the accounts. Just want to make sure you know that.*

Oh, hello. I did not expect this news. I'm wide awake now.

Me: *Perfect. When?*

Heath: *Let's meet for lunch and I'll show you the projections and answer any questions you have in person.*

Projections? He better have meant projectile—as in the money being projectile deposited back into the bank.

Me: *What do you mean by projections?*

Heath: *It means my downline is growing and good things are happening. Way ahead of schedule. Let's get together. Meet me at Ninfa's at one?*

Me: *Have you lost your mind? Did you seriously think I'd be willing to sit through your fucking sales pitch? And buy you lunch?*

Heath: *I can buy my own lunch. Soon I'll be able to buy anything I want. Anything you want too. I'm going to give you the world, I promise. It just takes time to grow a business.*

Me: *We were already growing a business. A REAL business, you fuckwit! One with expenses that you stuck me with after you STOLE money from it!!!!!!*

Heath: *Are you calling me a thief? I'm a signer on the account. I made those withdrawals legally.*

Me: *You actually didn't! They were business funds that you used for personal purposes!*

Heath: *No, I used them for a new business opportunity. People withdraw money from one business to start another one all the time.*

Me: *Profits! You can do that with profits. Not operating capital! Not the payroll account! You can't drain one business to launch another one. How can that possibly seem logical to you?*

Heath: *This is why I want you to sit down with me so I can show you the hard numbers.*

Me: *Here's a hard FACT. That money was not yours to take and invest elsewhere. I will pursue legal action if you don't return it.*

Heath: *I honestly don't see how we can remain business partners at this point.*

Me: *Are you saying you want to walk away from the franchise? Why couldn't you have just asked me to buy you out and given me a chance to look into that before you put us in this financial bind?*

Heath: *Sometimes you have to take risks to succeed. I tried to get you involved but you wouldn't listen. Offers don't stay on the table forever. You have to strike while the iron's hot.*

Oh, I'd like to strike him with a hot iron right now.

Me: *I've already got a call in to Marlise. As soon as I hear back from her, I'll let you know how we're going to proceed.*

Heath: *I guess you were serious about wanting to dissolve our personal relationship then.*

I literally can't. Did he really just state that like some kind of threat? I've been calling him the dumbass, but how dumb was my ass for dating him? There's no way he was this stupid when we met. I toss the phone back on my nightstand and lie in a stupor. Minutes pass before my phone buzzes again. As a testament to my own stupidity, I reach for it.

Heath: *I'll take your silence as confirmation. Just put all my stuff in a box and set it on your porch. I'll swing by later to get it.*

Me: *What stuff?*

Heath: *My blue Under Armor hoodie. My black Yeti tumbler that you took. My phone charger. The electric razor I keep in your bathroom and the protein bars I put in your pantry. I want what's left in the open box and the two unopened boxes. But if you ate any from the open box, that's fine. You don't have to replace them. Just put it all on your porch.*

He kept a running fucking list? Lord, give me strength. The last thing this boy wants to do is come over here today.

Me: *I do not have your hoodie. No idea what Yeti tumbler you're even talking about. As far as the rest of your insignificant shit, I'm busy. When I have time to put it in a box, I'll let you know!*

I genuinely don't have his hoodie. I'm keeping the Yeti and the phone charger, donating the razor, and crumbling every last protein bar into the trash like an offering to the garbage gremlins that apparently started eating my brain the moment I met him.

TWELVE
SEEKING COUNSEL AND QUESE

I grab my phone to check the time and the first thing I see is a message from Wick. He sent it an hour ago. Why does he wake up so early on a Saturday? It's barely eight. The gym parking lot is probably full. I rub my eyes and sit up to read his message.

Wick: *Send me your address. I'm picking you up at three. We'll come back to my place and soak for a while, shower, and then I'll help you work out the rest of your soreness before I take you to dinner.*

Me: *As enticing as your itinerary sounds, my day's booked.*

I'm meeting Marlise at her home office in a few hours. After I spill the whole embarrassing situation and listen to her wise legal advice, I'm coming home to drown my sorrows in junk food and reality TV binge-watching. Probably some true crime, too. No hot tub, no showering or working out my soreness in Wick's bed. Today, I'm hiding from the world, after I lay my soul bare to an attorney who doesn't pull any punches. My self-esteem will be battered but I deserve it. I need her blunt honesty as much as her expertise.

Wick: *Winner gets to choose. Loser can't refuse. I'm cashing in. Your address, please.*

Me: *Pretty sure I already paid up.*

Wick: *Not possible since I just decided the prize.*
Me: *Taking me to dinner? Shouldn't I have to take you to dinner?*
Wick: *All you have to do is let me be nice to you.*
Me: *I don't remember the stakes being that high.*
Wick: *Your address, please.*

I swing my legs over the side of the bed, let my feet meet the floor, and stand up. Oh, whoa. My body feels like it spent the night being tumbled inside a cement mixer. Yeah, I'll take him up on that hot tub offer. I send him my address, and hobble to the shower.

The hot water cascading down my back is soothing but I can't lie, I'd much rather be submerged in a hot tub.

Drying off after my shower takes a humbling amount of effort. Bending over, reaching around—someone needs to invent a body dryer that you can just stand in front of for a few minutes and be done. I'll invest. Sign me up. *Oops, never mind! I forgot all my money's tied up in porpoise placenta! Fucking Heath.* I ball up my towel and throw it in the corner of the bathroom, which is about as far as I could throw anything right now.

It's already ninety degrees outside but I'm drinking hot coffee anyway. Maybe I can warm my muscles from the inside out. I wish I had a foam roller here. Should've taken Heath's. He has one in every size and density option but he never uses them. There's got to be something here I could use. What do I have that would work?

I've got bolster pillows on my couch but they're way too soft. The pantry offers no viable options. Using a can of diced tomatoes would be painful. What about a wine bottle? It probably wouldn't break, right? But if it did . . . yeah, no to the wine bottle.

Oakley sounds half-asleep when she answers. "Did I wake you up?"

"No. It's freaking allergies. If I take meds, they knock me out. If I don't take them, I sound like this. What's up?"

"Do y'all have stretching equipment?"

"Ummm, equipment? If you mean like straps and rollers, yeah. If you're looking for a rack, we can't help you."

"Whatever. I still think y'all have a sex dungeon hidden somewhere in that house."

"Like I wouldn't tell you if we did. We're about to go grab some breakfast. Wanna meet us?"

"No. I have an appointment with Marlise in a few hours."

"Good. We'll drop off some implements of torture for you on our way back home. Say hi to my old apartment for me."

"Thanks. You're an angel, even though you sound more like a demon who smokes four packs a day right now."

"Hollis thinks my voice sounds sexy like this."

"He's just being nice so he can lure you into the dungeon. Enjoy your breakfast."

"Let me know what Marlise says."

"She's going to say I'm an idiot."

"Yeah, but then she'll say some helpful stuff."

"I can hardly wait."

I want to crawl back into my bed and ignore reality for one more hour, but if I do, there's no way I'll get back up. This was supposed to be my hide away day. Instead, I'm meeting with Marlise and then Wick, two people who most certainly aren't into letting people hide from them. More coffee, it is.

Marlise is on her back deck, sipping iced tea and admiring her potted jungle when I arrive. Walking up this driveway brings back memories. The garage apartment looks the same as it did when Oakley lived in it, but there's a new tenant now. I reach for the gate and Marlise shouts, "Get in here, girl! Let's hash this out and put a smile back on that pretty face. Nothing is ever as bad as it seems."

I appreciate her optimism, but this is every bit as bad as it seems.

She pours me some tea, and I try to lighten up a bit. "I guess if these plants survived Oakley, I can survive whatever I'm going through, huh?" I laugh but it's forced.

Marlise's smile is faint. "Eh, she only took out a few succulents." We both laugh at this. Oakley is a friend through thick and thin but she can kill a plant by looking at it sideways—a fact she didn't mention to Marlise when she agreed to water her plants while she was away.

"Good thing the ones out here were stronger," I say, taking the glass Marlise is offering before I sit down.

"Yeah, these are all hardy species. So are you." She taps her glass to mine. "Start talking."

She doesn't interrupt me once, just lets me dump the whole outrageous story without calling me an idiot or asking any questions. I finish and she still doesn't speak for a few moments. Her silence is unbearable. "Yeah, so, anyway, that's where I'm at."

Birds chirp. The water fountain in the center of the back yard burbles. Marlise slowly nods, still making no sound at all. I nearly leap out of my skin when a cricket hops from a plant behind me onto my shoulder. My convulsion flings it back into the foliage. Finally, she speaks. "It's not great, Nadine. But I've seen much worse. Hell, this isn't even the first multi-level marketing fiasco I've dealt with."

"Really?"

"Unfortunately, yes. It happens more often than you'd think. Those companies are slick. They say all the right things, produce impressive stats and charts, and make grand promises, but it's generally the same in the end."

"Okay. So, what do I do first?"

"First, you accept that he's not going to repay that money."

"I'd like to think he might."

"You're too damn smart to believe that. If he'd wised up and broken ties with the company he sank it into, then maybe I'd say there was a chance. But as long as he's bought in mentally, he's going to keep throwing more and more money at it. Every time he expresses a doubt, they'll dazzle him with some new bullshit, dangle another carrot."

"I still can't believe he got involved in this, let alone took the money. He wasn't a complete dumbass when we met, I swear."

"How many times a day do you find yourself saying or thinking that? It's because it's probably true. He wouldn't be the first reasonably intelligent person to get suckered in like this. Hell, a pipe dream is the easiest thing in the world to believe in. A fantasy sold as a lucky break, an amazing ground floor opportunity, a once-in-a-lifetime yada, yada." She rolls her hand through the air between us. "You get the gist. But you've got to remain level-headed and focused. You can't stay in business together. He will bleed you dry. And he won't even realize it's happening until it's over. He's in too deep, and if you don't want to hit rock bottom right along with him, you've got to get out by any means necessary."

"I don't even know where to begin, Marlise."

"That's why you're here. I do know. It might get ugly."

"It's already ugly. Walk me through what I need to do now and what I should expect next."

"You're not still sleeping with him, are you?"

"Are you kidding me? He basically fucking stole from me!"

"Women have kept sucking dicks after far worse behavior, trust me."

When I got out of my car here today, I didn't expect sucking dick to be a topic we'd cover. "Our personal relationship is completely dissolved. And I'm ready to get on with dissolving our business relationship."

"Don't be surprised if he suddenly wants to reconcile,

becomes once again charming, seems like the version of him you first met—"

"The version of him I first met wasn't draining my savings account. No man who owes me money is ever going to seem charming to me, especially not money I didn't voluntarily give him to begin with. I'm not sucking the dick of any guy who weakens my financial security. Not now, not ever! I bust my ass in a male-dominated industry and I don't take shit from any of the men I work with. I'm sure as fuck not going to become some guy's sex doll ATM machine while he chases rainbows looking for his imaginary pot of gold!"

"I always knew I liked you." She raises her iced tea glass again, takes a big drink, and says, "I'll review everything and make some phone calls. As soon as I know something, you'll know."

"What if he takes more money out of the accounts in the meantime?"

"Don't put in any more than you absolutely have to and watch it like a hawk. That's all you can do until we have our ducks in a row."

"I should probably tell you that I have it on good authority the other franchisee in Houston might be interested in buying our store. But I'd rather keep it if I can."

"That's a good ace in the hole. We'll keep it there for now. You got big plans tonight?"

"I'm supposed to have a date, but I'm going to cancel."

"I wouldn't. Where's he taking you?"

"First, to his place so we can soak in his hot tub and then to dinner."

"Hot tub first? Interesting."

"He's a personal trainer. Heath's personal trainer to be exact, but he was paid up for a few months so I decided those sessions belong to me now. And I'm sore from our last workout."

"Oh, I definitely like you. And you should definitely keep that date."

"I'll try not to make any rash decisions until I've had lunch and a nap."

"Good idea. Be safe going home. You know how to reach me if you need me. Otherwise, I'll be in touch early next week."

"Thanks."

Marlise waves as I close the gate behind me. A little red Mazda pulls in, rolls past me, and keeps going all the way back to the apartment. The driver, who I assume is the new tenant, looks so young. She couldn't have found a better place to live, that's for sure.

There's a bag on my porch. It's two short foam rollers, one smooth and one with knobby things on it to make me cry, and a canvas stretching strap. They're all brand new. *Dammit, Oakley.* I should've thought to just go buy my own gear. My brain isn't functioning at full capacity.

UNTITLED

The bottom of the bag is warm. They brought me food, too? I unpack everything on my kitchen counter. Chicken verde enchiladas and queso. Yes! I love my best friend. Everything is a mess, but I still have her. And queso.

THIRTEEN
NAKED AND AFRAID

It's not until after I've folded the bathing suit and put it in my bag that it hits me how weird it might seem to wear a suit in his hot tub today after wearing nothing in it the first time. Or maybe not? I stand in the middle of my bedroom and laugh at myself. Nothing makes sense.

Wick shows up right on time. I see him pulling up and I head for the front door, but when I open it, he's getting out of his car. *Was he coming to the door to get me like we're headed to prom? That's so cute.*

"I saw you pull up," I say, walking out. "But if I hadn't, you could've just texted to say you were here."

I lock my front door, and when I turn around, he's pointing at it. "What are you hiding behind there? Did you steal some monkeys from the Dallas Zoo?"

"At this point, who hasn't stolen animals from the Dallas Zoo?"

"Right? They're kind of going through it lately."

"I only have one monkey behind this door, and I didn't steal him."

"Oh, good. At least you have one monkey. I was starting to worry you were too normal."

"Normal? You think I'm normal?"

"Well, you're not a monkey thief so I guess that's a check in the normal column."

"That's a pretty low bar for normal."

"I've got a pretty high tolerance for weird."

"Hang on to it. It'll come in handy if you spend much more time around me."

"Are you sore?"

"Not as bad as after our first workout, but yeah."

I swear his smile looks proud. I'd be sore even if I'd done all those squats on my own. Well, now that he's shown me how to do them correctly. Okay, fine. Credit where credit's due, I guess.

His house smells good, like it's been freshly cleaned. Not that it smelled bad before, but I bet he uses a housekeeping service. He leads me into his room and tosses me a neatly rolled, navy-and-white-striped towel from a wicker basket. I used a towel from his bathroom last time, but he definitely had one like this wrapped around his waist. All the towels in the basket match but they're not his bath towels. They're over-sized, like beach towels, which explains why they're next to his bedroom door instead of in the bathroom—easy to grab on his way out to the hot tub. I bring the fluffy towel I'm holding up to my nose and inhale without thinking. It smells fresh, too, no lingering scent of chlorine.

"Did you honestly think I'd give you a dirty towel?"

"No, it's not that. I love the smell of clean laundry. I swear I do that to my own towels every time I take one out of the cabinet." *How normal do I seem now?* "Whatever detergent you use smells really good. What is it?"

"I'd have to go to the laundry room and look."

"Cleaning service. I knew it."

"Interesting."

"What's interesting?"

"The fact that you're so curious about the details of my life."

"I'm not."

"You were obviously speculating about whether or not I used a cleaning service."

"That's a totally normal thing to wonder about when you come into someone's house for the first time and it's hospital-level clean."

"Is it? I've never wondered about it." He pulls his shirt over his head, and my eyes trace the muscles being revealed.

"That's because you're a man." I step out of my sandals, and glance at my overnight bag I've set on his bed. It holds two choices of outfits for dinner, one more casual than the other since I don't know where we're going yet, and a bathing suit I'm still deciding if I'm going to wear today.

"What gave it away?" He takes his shorts and boxers down together. No modesty. Not that he has anything to be modest about with his dick noticeably at half-staff as he tosses his clothes on a chair before wrapping a towel around his waist. If there weren't kids living next door, I'm quite sure he'd walk outside completely naked. "You don't want to get undressed in front of me, do you?"

"I know that probably seems strange at this point but—"

"You don't have to explain. I'll be in the kitchen." He smiles, and then he turns to go. "Feel free to smell my clothes all you want."

"I'm not smelling your clothes, you weirdo!"

"Whatever you say." His voice trails off down the hall.

Moment of truth: to suit up, or go bare? I set my towel on the bed and unzip my bag.

With the towel securely wrapped around my body, I fold my clothes and set them in my bag. On top of my bathing suit.

Wick looks up from his phone when I walk into his kitchen. "That towel looks good on you."

I shield my face with my forearm like a celebrity trying to deny the paparazzi. "No pictures, please."

He laughs, and the soothing tone of it instantly relaxes me. We walk outside. No wine this time. Just me and my aching muscles, following him to the hot tub, and ducking under the privacy screen. Wick turns the handle to lower the screen all the way. I drop my towel on the small table I didn't notice before, and climb in while he's occupied. I slide to the bench. It dips lower than the corner seats, and my body is nearly completely submerged. He climbs in and moves toward me. "Can I sit by you?"

"You asked that like we're kids on a school bus."

"Listen, I was smooth on the bus."

"Oh, yeah? Show me your bus moves."

"Okay. What grade are we in?"

I crack up. "How early did you start perfecting your moves?"

He sits next to me, and drapes an arm across the ledge behind my shoulders. "In the third grade, I asked this little girl named Olivia if she wanted to sit with me and share my gummy worms."

"That's just sweet. That's not a move."

"The day before, I'd seen her ask another boy if she could have one of his gummy worms. He said no, told her he was really hungry. She asked again, told him those were her favorite snack. He still said no."

"You opportunistic little player!"

He shrugs, that cocky smirk on full display. "What can I say? I've been fulfilling female desire since a young age."

"Uh-huh, yeah. I'm sure it was *all* about her. What did you get in exchange for your gummy worms? Your first kiss?"

"No. She had this head full of blond curly hair. Every day I walked past her and all I could think about was how much I wanted to touch it, but I already knew it would be weird to touch a girl's hair without her permission. Not to mention, I'd probably get in trouble for not keeping my hands to myself, but I was dying to touch those curls."

"Aw, you just wanted to see how her hair felt? Okay, that's still kinda sweet."

"I wanted to pull it and see if it would stay straight or bounce back into a curl when I let it go."

"Did you pull that little girl's hair?"

"No, she outsmarted me. I told her what I wanted to do, so she stretched a section of her hair until it was straight and showed me that, yes, it would go right back to being curly. Then she told me I could do it as long as I didn't pull her hair, which kept me busy the rest of the bus ride. While she ate every one of my gummy worms."

"Good for her. I hope little curly-haired Olivia is doing well."

"She's a divorce attorney now. I'm sure she gets her clients everything they want."

"Again, good for her. So, do you still have a thing for curly hair?"

"Curly, straight, I'm not so curious about hair anymore. But bees? I'm really intrigued by bees." He leans in and his fingertip traces the flight pattern of my tattoo, extending it to dip below the water's surface and loop-de-loop around my nipple. And then his mouth is on mine, and I'm the one who escalates the kiss to a ravenous level. He pinches my nipple, increasing the pressure like he did the first time we sat in his hot tub together, but now, I know what to expect when he lets go. My breath quickens in anticipation of the rush, but unlike before, the anxiousness is because I'm looking forward to it.

I turn toward him and nearly straddle his thigh. The fingers of his free hand thread into my hair and he folds them down to pull. His hand is close to my scalp and it hurts a little. I want him to pull harder. Pinch harder. He does both. And when he lets go, he does it simultaneously, and my body goes slack at the release.

He pulls me all the way onto his thigh and keeps kissing me with his arms wrapped around me, preventing me from sliding right off his lap and going under. He's spread his legs to ensure I'm straddling only one. His firm thigh feels good under my soft pussy. So good. Our kiss intensifies again and I rock shamelessly against his leg. He tightens his quads and presses up, encouraging me. He's relaxed me; now he wants to get me off, but I'm not sure I care about that yet.

The way his hard muscles are palpating my clit isn't strong enough to make me come, but it still feels incredible, and I want to keep feeling it. Just pleasure, no obligation or expectation . . . his tongue duels with mine, and he massages the back of my neck while I continue to ride his leg. This is needy and desperate. Obscene. And I love it.

My clit swelling until the teasing pressure is no longer comfortable. I break our kiss and look into his eyes.

"You want more?" he asks, knowingly.

"Yes," I admit, pressing my forehead to his.

He stands and I wrap my legs around his waist while he turns us, but when he tries to set me on the side of the hot tub, I keep my legs wrapped. "I'll fall," I say.

"You won't. I promise." He holds me securely in his arms and lowers me all the way to the edge. "Spread your legs and lean back. I've got you."

I spread my legs but stay upright. His arms stay in place behind my back.

"Lean," he says again, tipping me a little. "Take me with you." I don't understand what he envisions but I'm pretty sure we'll both go over the edge if I go back too far. I only tilt a little. His arms tighten and support me. "Keep going."

When I extend farther, it pulls him up from the water a little, and he immediately bends down to kiss my clit. His arms are solid across my lower back. This still seems like a dangerous idea, but the only way to increase his access is to elevate my hips, so I exhale and recline until his arms lock, alerting me that I've hit the limit. My back arches and I let my head fall back. I feel completely supported. Precarious, but safe-ish.

He flattens his tongue and it begins performing the detail work his thigh couldn't quite accomplish. Damn, I forgot the exhilaration of doing something just because you could, never mind if you should. Physically, anyway. I may have made other types of questionable decisions recently, but I don't think I'm going to regret this one. My pelvis lurches of its own accord when his tongue circles my clit. He takes the hint and by the time he closes his mouth on it and begins to suck, I'm already halfway there.

It's only when my orgasm wanes and I'm quivering through the aftershocks that I realize I've fallen so far back the top of my head is nearly touching his deck, and he's practi-cally standing. He pulls me back up to sit on the edge and I sway. It's dizziness, but he smiles with that egotistical slant, like it's all him. I return the smile while the blood continues to rush back into my veins. He's responsible for enough of my current physical impairment that he might deserve to gloat a bit. That was definitely my first headstand orgasm.

I rest my forehead against his and whisper. "Holy saint of dangerous sex acts, that was amazing."

"There should definitely be a saint for that."

An alarm sounds. His phone is on the same table where I dropped my towel. He puts me safely on the bench, and then he wades to the edge and climbs out to silence his phone.

Holding a towel open for me, he says, "Time to get out."

"You're taking mercy on my knees today?"

"You give me far too much credit." He wraps me up as I step out. "We need to get dried off because we're about to have visitors."

"What do you mean visitors?"

"You'll see."

His doorbell rings as we walk inside, and he keeps right on

going toward the front door. "You're going to open the door wearing nothing but a towel?"

"They expect us to be naked."

"I'm sorry. What?" I stay in the kitchen.

He opens the door and says hi, welcomes someone inside. I can't see who's coming in, but the replying voices are female. Two female voices. I don't know what he thinks is about to happen here but I will get a ride so fast it makes his head spin. "Yeah, set up in my room," he says. "It's at the end of hall."

Set up what, exactly?

Wick comes back into the kitchen. "They need a few minutes. We should probably drink some water first."

"Before what?"

"Massages. You didn't recognize the tables they're carrying?"

"I couldn't see them from here." I take a sip from the glass of water he's set in front of me. "You scheduled a couple's massage?"

"Are you anti-massage?"

"No. I'm just confused."

"You didn't know you could hire massage therapists to come to your house?"

"I did, but I've never done it. Do you hire them often?"

"They're professionals, I promise. I've gotten massages from both of them. I usually go to the spa where they work, but since you were already coming over to use the hot tub, I figured it'd be easier to have them come here. Then we can shower and get ready to go to dinner without having to get dressed in between, or if you'd rather take a nap first, we can do that and then shower . . ." He's eying me like I'm the one who's done something suspicious.

"Why didn't you tell me this was going to happen?"

"I thought it might be a nice surprise?"

"How long ago did you book it?"

"Yesterday."

"That's pretty short notice."

"The spa closes at five on Saturdays. I figured there was a chance they wouldn't all have late afternoon clients so I called to see if there were two therapists who'd be able to take a home appointment. And it worked out. Sometimes that happens. Things work out."

"I don't mean to seem ungrateful. It's just a lot."

"You have control issues. That's your problem."

"Did you mean skills? Because, yes, I have control skills." I smile at him over the rim of the glass before I take another drink.

"I won the bet, Nadine. You have to let me be nice to you."

"For how much longer?"

"Until I'm done."

"That seems excessive."

"I like doing things to excess." He winks.

Before I can respond, one of the women appears from around the corner and says they're ready for us.

I sneak nervous glances at Wick as we follow her back down the hall. This just feels like such a *couple* thing to do. I mean, it's called a *couple's massage* for a reason. We're not a couple. We're just two people—who, so far, have spent more time together with our clothes off than with them on. I'm sure dinner won't be weird at all.

FOURTEEN
WHAT'S ONE MORE NIGHT?

"So, am I winning for the best date ever yet?" Wick asks when he comes back into his room after seeing the massage therapists out.

I'm sitting on the end of his bed, wrapped in a fresh towel and completely zoned out. "I mean, best *ever*? You're kind of shooting for the stars there."

"I guess it's a good thing this date's not over yet. You ready to shower and go to dinner or do you want to take a nap?"

"Shower. If I nap after that massage, I won't get up for dinner. But we're not showering together."

"Perfect. You shower. I'll nap. Wake me up when you're done in the bathroom."

"Are you really going to crawl into your bed with all that oil on your body?"

"I toweled off." He holds out his arm and looks at it. "I'm good. Enjoy your shower."

"You know I'm going to use all the hot water, right?"

"Me taking a cold shower before dinner will probably work in your favor." He drops his towel, and slides between his sheets. "Unless you're more of an exhibitionist than I thought."

"I'm definitely not."

"Challenge accepted." He fluffs his pillows and rolls over with his back to me.

I check out all the products in his shower. His body wash scent is called whiskey barrel. Smells like smoky vanilla to me. Smells good on him, regardless. The shampoo is minty. There's a bar of soap that's heavy on the eucalyptus. I figure this strong soap will probably take the oil off my skin quicker than my gentle body wash so I lather up the washcloth. Wow! That's a powerful scent. My sinuses are clear now. I try a tiny amount of his body wash to see how the combination smells. Much milder. The water's still hot when I reluctantly turn it off.

My muscles all feels loose and lazy, but that soap was an eye-opener. I take my time drying my hair, mostly because I don't have the energy to hurry, but I also don't want to ruin this relaxed feeling.

I open the bathroom door slowly, and step back into his room, expecting to find him asleep but he's staring right at me. "I was trying not to wake you up."

"How was your shower?"

"Good. How was your nap?"

"Short. Did you leave me any hot water?"

"I did. Where are we going for dinner?"

"Maybe that's another surprise."

"Maybe you better rethink that so I know what to wear."

"I like the way you wear my towels."

"Most restaurants would frown on that choice."

"Nude restaurants are a thing. I wonder if Houston has one."

"I'm not dining naked in public."

"But if I had food delivered?"

"Where are we going?"

"How about you wear whatever feels most comfortable, and tell me what you're hungry for. Think about it while I'm in the shower." He leaves his bed, and casually strolls past me on his way to the bathroom. If he went to dinner naked, I bet we'd get excellent service.

I stare at the spot in the bed he's just vacated. It's probably still warm. Shaking away the thought, I force myself to get dressed.

His shower is quick. "Did you decide where we're going?"

"I'm about to do that thing men hate and say I don't know what I want."

"I don't hate it. We're not in a hurry. We can just drive until something looks good."

"Are you serious?"

"Why not? There are hundreds of restaurants in this town. But let's make it a rule that we have to pick somewhere neither one of us has ever been."

"Okay. But you better pick an area with plenty of places close together. Otherwise, we could end up driving all night and having to hit a drive-through for burgers after everything else is closed."

"Whatever happens, happens."

"Does anything upset you?"

"Very little these days." He zips up a pair of jeans that fit him so perfectly I can't help but stare. "I used to get upset pretty easily. Never helped anything."

"Feels good to get pissed off sometimes, though."

"Does it?" He shakes his head no in answer to his own question before slipping his arms into a shirt with short sleeves that hug his biceps. When he has it buttoned up, it's chef's-kiss snug across his chest without being tight. Wick's not huge, not bulked up by any means, but he is in great shape. Lots of very well-defined shapes.

"All I know is I feel better after I rage and get all the anger out of my system."

He laughs. "All you little-bitty women are always feisty."

"I'm not little-bitty. I may be thin but I'm tall."

"You're average height at best. But I like that you see your-self as tall. You're like that meme of the kitten looking in the mirror and seeing a lion."

"I am nobody's kitten."

"You know I have to call you that now, right? Kitten."

"Congratulations. My vagina just super-glued itself shut. That's how I feel about that nickname."

He smiles, sits on the end of the bed to put on his socks, and whispers, "Feisty."

I throw a pillow at his head, and then zip up my bag and hook it over my shoulder. He turns to toss the pillow back at me and stops. "Why are you taking your bag? You know you're going to stay here tonight."

"Just because I stayed last time doesn't mean I'm staying tonight. We drank a lot of wine last time."

"There will probably be wine with dinner."

"You're taking me home after dinner."

"That's the plan."

"To *my* home."

"So, you're saying I should pack a bag?"

"Just because you're quick doesn't mean you're funny."

He stands and walks close enough to grab my hips and pulls me forward. "But you're smiling." He strokes my cheek with the backs of his fingers. "And you're beautiful. I will drive you to Galveston for seafood, to San Antonio for Mexican food, hell, I'll take you all the way to Louisiana for gumbo, if that's what you want. But drop the bag, because no matter where we go, I'm bringing you back home with me."

I hear my bag hit the floor before I even realize my shoulder has sloped to set it free. He calls my smile beautiful but his apparently has magical powers. "We can get all that food in Houston, you know?"

"I was making a point."

"False promises." I tsk and shake my head. "Should've known."

"Try me."

"Shut up and buy me a steak."

"You never disappoint."

"You just haven't known me long enough."

"True. I wish I'd met you a long time ago." He squeezes my ass so hard my heels leave the floor, and kisses my neck so softly my reluctance to stay the night leaves my body. "Let's get out of here before we starve."

It doesn't take long to find a place neither of us has tried. It's not a fancy steakhouse but I pull up the menu online and confirm they do have steaks. The reviews are good and you don't need a reservation.

Inside, it's comfortable. The lighting isn't so dim you can't see the menu, the booths aren't stiff, and the waitstaff doesn't have to tell you where every ingredient was sourced. Their steaks look good but I can't resist the grilled sea bass. Wick orders a ribeye.

"Mister Fitness doesn't even opt for a lean cut," I tease.

"I don't eat a lot of red meat, but when the craving hits, I want all the fat."

"Yeah, that's like me and ice cream. Sometimes, sorbet's just not gonna work."

He does a spit take with his water. "Exactly the same."

As he predicted, there is wine with dinner but my stomach's not empty, so I never feel anything more than a soft buzz. It's nice. Everything about this is nice. Easy.

He's good company, in so many ways.

When we're back in his car with all our food cravings exceedingly satisfied, I don't raise any arguments about staying with him tonight. He leans in to kiss me before he backs out and he tastes like the raspberry sauce on the chocolate cake we split for dessert. Smells good, tastes good . . . what's one more night?

～

In his bed with moonlight slipping in between the partially open blinds, our naked bodies intertwined and rumpling his sheets, I can sense his frustration when I shy away from attempts at intimacy. When he rocks his hips slowly, I thrust mine upward sooner and sooner to encourage a faster pace. When his kiss travels up from my neck to find my lips, I turn away. When the backs of his fingers begin to stroke my cheek, I reach for his hand but he grabs my wrist instead. He clasps both of my wrists in his hands and stretches my arms above my head, pinning them there, the weight of his body crushing mine into the mattress. "Stop it. Look at me."

I make eye contact and immediately regret it. His are shining in the scant light, and the peaks of his cheekbones, the cut of his jaw, all his edges are silhouetted like a sin-soaked image from the hottest scene in a movie. But his voice is soft. "It doesn't always have to be rough."

"That's the only way I like it."

"No, that's a shield you use to shut out feeling anything that isn't purely physical. Raw and rough is great, but it's not all there is, Nadine. Let tonight be more."

"I don't want more."

"Well, I do."

"Fine. You want me to just lie here and let you make love to me?"

"Sure. Just lie there. Don't enjoy it at all." He rolls his hips with his cock buried inside me. "No response, no matter what I do . . ." He goes back to kissing my neck.

"That wasn't a challenge, Wick."

"It is now." His mouth travels down to my chest, kissing and biting as he continues, until he claims my nipple.

Damn, he's good. My wrists are still in his hands and his grip tightens as he sucks harder. Whose rule book does he think he's playing by? Because this is exactly the way I want it. If he'd just fuck me harder. But that's the part he won't give me, and there isn't enough space between our hips for me to move the way I want. Or move at all. His strokes are long and slow, and the contrast between that and everything else he's doing feels like a trick, like some sleight of hips illusion he thinks I won't notice because he has me entranced elsewhere.

Okay, this I can agree to. I didn't know he was proposing a combo package. Why can't he just tell me things instead of having to show me to prove a point? He's the one with control issues. Stubborn ass.

The moment I give in and relax, he lunges up to kiss me. And there's no denying him this kiss. His dick is still pulling long strokes and my pussy is responding like he's pumping a well. He squeezes my wrists and my walls squeeze in on him.

This kiss is passionate, and his thrusts are gaining momentum, now that I've given him control. Every touch, every stroke, everything, everything is crashing at the intersection of lust and adoration, and I need to be able to move my hips because this is too much to take lying still.

I'm squirming and whimpering into his mouth. He releases one of my wrists briefly but his other hand grabs it and clenches them both together while he reaches down to rub my clit, putting enough space between us that I'm free to move beneath him. But now that I have the freedom, I don't want it. If I move, I'll change the way he's stroking my clit and there's already a flicker building in my core. He has me exactly where he wants me. And it's exactly where I want to be. He's absolutely a magician and I hate him and need him and want him and oh, damn . . . my thighs tremble, and he bites my bottom lip. I bite back and we're devouring each other when my pussy starts to quiver and my spine arches. "Oh, yes. Yes, yes, yes."

I drench his sheets, and he shortens his strokes, buries his face in my hair, and groans into my ear like he's breaking a vow of chastity. "Fuck, this tight little snatch is soooo damn gooood." He slams into me as he empties his load. After panting against my shoulder for a minute, he looks up and smiles, sweat beading on his forehead.

"Okay, fine. You broke me."

"I'd never try to break you. I just want to break down the walls you put up."

"They're down. Crumbled. Rubble. Ground to dust in some places."

"You're just saying that to flatter me."

"You flatter yourself plenty."

He kisses me. It's sweeter than I want it to be, but I don't want it to end. I'm broken. Crumbled.

FIFTEEN
RUNNING ON EMPTY

Same traffic jam, different freeway. Every day this week, I've spent half my time on the road sitting still, waiting for an accident to be cleared up ahead. And this is bad because when I'm not moving, my mind doesn't have to stay focused on the cars around me. It can drift back to last weekend with Wick. The hot tub, the massage, dinner, the intimacy he tricked me into . . . . it's a wonder I haven't ended up causing a wreck of my own.

The last time a man felt this right this soon, we both got hurt in the end. And then along came Heath, who was never supposed to be anything more than a good time. He really was a good time for a while, back before the jellyfish jizz. Now, he's a liability that requires legal intervention. And Jayce is in Alaska. It's where he's meant to be, I know that. But I rarely have *what might've been* thoughts about him anymore. Wick makes me think about a lot of things I'd rather keep buried and never feel again.

It doesn't help that I've been in and out of refineries all week, and while most of the men I deal with in them are great, there's always that one misogynistic asshole who has to say something that makes me think losing my job would be worth it just to jam a spiked heel right in his cajónes. And then my brain starts making comparisons between some men and others . . .

My screen shows an incoming call from Oakley and I breathe a sigh of relief. This is the distraction I need.

"Hey, what are you up to?" I ask, knowing she's probably stuck in traffic in some other part of town.

"Are you keeping an eye on this storm?"

"You mean the one blowing through my life?"

"No, the one that just blew into the Gulf and became a hurricane."

"Oh, shit. I had no idea."

"If it gets much bigger, you need to pack a bag, and come stay with us."

"Calm down, Mom. We're fifty miles from the coast. We'll be fine."

"Right now. But if it gains strength, we could have massive flooding. There could be tornadoes. We have the wine cellar."

"Oh, yeah, that's just where I want to be when a tornado hits, in a room full of glass bottles."

"That are all filled with wine." She laughs. "Seriously, though. We have two generators that will run the whole house if we lose power, and our place has more safe spaces in a storm than your duplex."

"Are you saying I might finally get to see the dungeon?"

"There is no dungeon."

"What's this hurricane's name?"

"Nadine."

Dammit, how does she always turn up to make me laugh at just the right time? A hurricane named after me right now would feel like an honor. "For real, what is it?"

"It's really Hurricane Nadine. Now do you see why I'm so worried?"

"Be right back, changing my name on all my socials and having t-shirts made."

"Garth says he's coming to brunch on Sunday."

"I'll check with my hurricane and get back to y'all." Garth is Oakley's coworker, but over the past few years, we've all become friends, brunch buddies when he can be bothered to show. His weekends are eventful, and not just with the company events they host. "If I ever make it home. Where are you at?"

"Almost home. You seeing your trainer in the morning?"

"No. I've had three sessions already this week."

"How many outside the gym?"

"None. My schedule's been full. No time for dinner dates."

"You still have to eat."

"Evenings with him turn into mornings with him."

"Maybe he wants to come to brunch on Sunday, too."

"Nice try. He won't be there."

"Stay safe on the road."

"Stay safe in the dungeon. Bye."

The low fuel light comes on as I pull onto my driveway. No way am I backing out to get gas. That's a tomorrow problem. Right now, all I care about is food and sleep.

I set my laptop on the kitchen table and take out my phone to order dinner. I'll probably do a little work before my food arrives, and probably a little more while I eat. Before I even bring up my delivery options, a call comes in.

It's Marlise. A call from an attorney after business hours? This is either going to be very good news, or very bad news. There's no in-between. "Hi, Marlise."

"Well, I said when I knew something, you'd know."

"Hold on. Let me sit down for this."

"The good news is you're a partnership and not an LLC. Removing a member from an LLC in Texas can be a lot more complicated."

"That's why you talked me out of forming one, isn't it? It wasn't just because neither one of us owned property so we didn't need one. You saw this coming."

"I've seen a lot of young men with dollar signs in their eyes. Some have the drive to make it happen, and others just have a rich fantasy life. Let's say Heath struck me as more of a dreamer than a doer. But you are a go-getter. And you're smart, which is why I know you can understand that sometimes we have to make hard choices."

"And what are my choices right now?"

"You can either sell the franchise, or if Heath will agree to it without making things difficult, you can buy him out right now. If he's not agreeable, you can still buy him out, but it'll take a little longer. It's all stipulated in the buy and sell agreement. He's clearly in breach of the partnership, but that doesn't mean he won't try to contest it and drag it out. Corporate will allow the other franchisee in town to buy your store, by the way. It would make for a quick sale."

"If Heath thinks he can get money out of the deal, he'll be more than agreeable. I'd be able to keep the franchise as a sole proprietorship? They won't force me to sell to get rid of Heath?"

"Correct. But do you have the money to buy him out? If it means taking on more debt, I really think you should consider selling. You're in an unusually favorable position for such a new business."

"Do you have firm numbers, including the fees to change the franchise agreement? And your fee, of course. I want to know exactly how much I'd need." In my mind, I see Nicholas from the bank with his concerned expression, and his guarded voice telling me what a credit risk I've become. It's not fair that my back is against the wall like this. The juice bar makes money. There has to be a way I can make this work.

"Why don't you come sit down with me next week so we can go over all the details. Wednesday afternoon work for you?"

"I can make it work."

"Two o'clock?"

"I'll be there."

Again, before I can order dinner, the phone rings in my hand. It's our manager at Skweez, Tori. "Hey, Tori. What's up?"

"Hey. Um, I stepped outside to call you because I don't want everyone to hear this but, Heath just left, and I think you should know about these stickers."

"What stickers?"

"He gave a box of stickers to the new girl and told her we're supposed to put them on all the cups. She came to me after he left to ask if she should do that now or keep stocking the cooler."

"Please tell me they are not stickers with the Bounty of the Seas logo on them."

"It's a QR code."

"That goes to a website for that shit?"

"Yeah. And when the site first opens, there's a pop-up window that shows Heath's picture and a message making it sound like it's endorsed by Skweez. There's some creative wording."

"Keep those stickers in the box. Do not let anyone defile a single happy lemon! I'm on my way." This idiot's going to get himself sued by corporate. He's going to get us both sued by corporate.

Guess I'm buying gas tonight after all. What if Tori wouldn't have been there? How many people would've scanned that sticker? He's going to get our franchise terminated before I even have a chance to buy him out!

~

I park behind Skweez, and I'm shocked to see how busy the store is when I walk in. A crowd like this on a Thursday night would normally make me happy, but the only thing that could quell my anger tonight is putting Heath's head through a juicer. I manage a smile for the employees as Tori introduces me to the new girl.

Grabbing a couple premade juice blends from the cooler, I give Tori the sign to meet me out back. She's already put the stickers in her car because she's a gem. Given how hectic things are inside, I'm hopeful no one noticed her carrying them out, but I'm sure the new girl has already told someone about the weird stickers Heath gave her, and they'll all be gossiping about it by closing time.

Tori sighs when she hands over the box. "I'm sorry I had to call you this late. I know you have a full-time job, and I considered waiting until tomorrow, but my gut said to tell you as soon as possible."

"You did the right thing. I needed to know about this tonight."

"Is everything okay with the store, Nadine? I mean, I can tell something has happened with you and Heath, but like, are our jobs safe?"

"Yeah, the store's fine. It's all good, I promise. Heath is going through some stuff. I can't go into detail, but if he does anything else like this, call me. No matter the time. Always call me." I put myself in her shoes for a moment. Yeah, I'd be looking for new job as soon as the sun came up tomorrow. Our employees can't be exposed to the bullshit going on between me and Heath. He's got to stay out of the store. But how in the hell can I enforce that when he's still an owner?

I sit in my car and drink my juice after Tori goes back inside. It occurs to me I haven't checked the bank balances today, and my heart races. Paula is also keeping an eye on them but I need to see for myself that he hasn't pulled two stupid human tricks in one day. The money's fine. He's not completely running amok. These stickers are going straight in the trash.

No. No, they're going somewhere else entirely.

SIXTEEN
NEGOTIATIONS CONTINUE

I 'm covering the last sliver of gray paint that's still visible when Heath comes up the stairs and spots me at his door. "What the hell are you doing?"

"Putting these QR codes in a much kinder place than where I'd like to stick them." I stand up and admire my handiwork. He wanted advertising? He's got it.

"You can't put stickers all over my front door! Are you insane?"

"Am *I* insane? Me? Did you really think you were going to get away with putting these on our cups?"

"It's not a big deal. It's just a sticker."

"If you really thought it was no big deal, then why'd you ask a brand-new employee to do your dirty work? She's young, cute, kind of shy . . . let me guess, you flirted a little, kept your voice low so nobody else could hear, and then you handed her that box like you were trusting her with some special task. Stop me when I go off-script."

"She's interested in Bounty of the Seas. She sees the potential, unlike some people."

"You are so bad at reading women. But so very good at

underestimating us. Thankfully, she took that box straight to Tori as soon as you left."

"She disobeyed a direct order from an owner of the company? She should be fired!"

"I'm giving her a raise, first thing tomorrow morning!"

"Maybe I need to take a more active role in how we run things."

"The fuck you do! All you need to take is my buyout offer."

"Which is what?" He holds out his hand like I should've shown up with a proposal at the ready.

"When I know, you'll know!"

"I hope you realize if any paint comes off with these stickers, you're repainting my whole door, Nadine." He starts picking at the edges of one. "So childish," he mutters.

He wants to see childish? I'll show him childish. The box flips over when I kick it, spilling the remaining stickers around his feet. I take the stairs two-at-a-time on my way down.

"This is going to take me all night!"

Stopping on the sidewalk below, I look up at him, and slap my hand over my heart. "Oh, no. Did someone else's behavior cause you an inconvenience? I can't begin to imagine your pain." He scowls in my direction. I flip him off with both middle fingers and my whole chest. "You can scrape at those stickers until your fingers bleed and days turn into weeks for all I care."

"You are such a bitch!"

I nod my head emphatically and do a shoulder roll that turns into a dance as I mock him. "Boss bitch. Bad bitch. Head bitch in charge. The bitch who kicked your sorry ass to the curb!" I stop dancing and stare at him. "But most importantly, I am the bitch you better stop testing before you hit my limits." I square my shoulders and walk away.

Two guys on a balcony whistle and clap.

A woman struggling to insert her key while her purse and

two bags of groceries hang from her wrist yells, "Get him, girl!"

Yeah, I'm going to get him, alright. Get him the fuck out of my business. Up there scratching at some stickers like a scared puppy, trying to get back in the house after he ate a shoe and shit on the rug. Or in his case, swallowed a load of jellyfish jizz and shit on his own life. And mine. Fucker.

When I get in my car, I take the sticker from my pocket and drop it into the center console. I don't know why I kept one; something just told me I should.

I ignored Wick's text inviting me to come in to the gym this morning. It's Saturday and I have laundry to do and reports to file and groceries to buy. I ignored his call last night, too.

But the email I just got from Marlise is harder to ignore. She sent me a text to be sure I knew it was in my inbox. The number staring back at me when I open it is in the ballpark of the amount I anticipated, but it still stings to look at in in black and white.

That's the price to be free of Heath but keep the store. The sole owner. Is it worth it? It's what I want. Can I accomplish it? Not via any responsible choices, but there is always someone willing to lend money. Will the terms be predatory? Probably. Am I considering it anyway? Oh, look, there's a text from Paula. My CPA is working through the weekend, too.

And there goes the buzzer on the dryer. I better go fold those towels. These women need to learn to take a day off. Monday will be here soon enough.

By the time the sun goes down, my house smells as clean as Wick's. I need to stop thinking about him and his house and his hot tub, but the only other thing I can think about is a large scary number. He probably already has a date. I've ignored him twice. Reaching out now will require an apology and an excuse, and I don't exactly excel at either of those things. But he excels at some things . . .

Me: *Hey, sorry I've been hard to reach. This week was crazy.*

Wick: *Oh, sure. Reach out after you've exhausted all your other options.*

Me: *It's down to you or bleaching the grout in my shower. Any chance I can interest you in a late dinner?*

Wick: *Did you just offer to cook me dinner?*

Wait, what? Shit.

Me: *I can open a jar of spaghetti sauce like nobody else.*

Wick: *On my way.*

That was easy. It'd be easier if I had a jar of spaghetti sauce in the pantry. I take inventory of what I have that could go on pasta: olive oil, garlic, tomatoes, onions . . . okay, so I guess I am cooking.

The onions are soft and the tomatoes are ready to go into the pan when Wick shows up. I dump them in and smile at the sizzle when they hit the oil, wipe my hands, and run to the door.

"Wow," he says. "You make jarred spaghetti sauce smell really good."

"What you smell is fresh onions, garlic, and tomatoes. And you're welcome."

"No fresh herbs?" He lifts the bottle of wine he's holding. "Do you at least have a cork screw?"

"I have three."

"Just in case the first two break."

"Precisely." I lead him into the kitchen.

"How'd you find this place?" he asks.

Definitely not about to tell him I was dating the landlord back then and didn't have to search it out. Everyone assumes I got some special deal but I didn't. I wouldn't have taken any special deal. Anyway, we stopped dating a few months after I moved in. But he's still my landlord, and guys tend to get weird, and sometimes say stupid shit when they find out that information. My tolerance for stupid comments is never high, but it's lower than usual right now. "I've been here a long time. It's old but it's definitely better than an apartment. I like only having to share walls with one neighbor. Plus, he travels for work so he's hardly ever home. And when he is in town, he's usually at his girlfriend's place. Nice guy, but I don't see him much."

"Perfect neighbor. You got lucky." The wine cork makes a satisfying pop as he pulls it free.

"Right place, right time." I strain the pasta and toss it in the pan with the sauce. "You good with fresh parmesan?"

"Love it." He finds my wine glasses on his own, just opens cabinets like he owns the place until he chooses the right door. I don't mind him making himself at home. His comfortable confidence puts me at ease, too. He's just always so damn easy to be around.

We sit on my couch with oily pasta and red wine, and I don't even care if we spill. Sometimes, I sweat the small stuff, maybe too often, but stains can be dealt with. Tonight, I only want to focus on time well spent with this gray-eyed man, who softens me when I'm feeling hard, who I don't mind slurping spaghetti in front of, whose fingers stroke my cheek after he wipes the corner of my mouth with his thumb. We came into the living room because we were going to watch TV while we ate, but the remote is still on the cushion next to my thigh where I set it down when he made me laugh before I even hit the power button.

Our dirty bowls on the coffee table don't bother me at all. The kitchen was so far away, and his lips were so close, and now mine are nearly numb from kissing him for so long and the wine is nearly gone and I am nowhere near ready for him to go. "Stay," I whisper.

"You'd have to kick me out to get me to leave."

He follows me into my bedroom, and begins to unbutton his shirt. I grip the hem of my tank top and start to lift it, but he says, "No. Let me undress you." I watch as he removes his shirt, revealing familiar muscles. When he's done removing all his own clothes, he walks toward me, and the shiver that hardens my nipples has nothing to do with the temperature in the room.

His hands meet my waist, and he lifts my tank top slowly over my head, pausing to appreciate my sheer bra, before he unbuttons my shorts. When they drop to the rug, he smiles. "Mmmm, the matching set. So sexy." Unfastening my bra single-handedly while his other delves into my panties to stroke my pussy, his eyes darken when the strap separates behind my back and his fingers glide through my slickness. I'm eager to feel them inside me, but I want to pleasure him first for once.

Looking into his eyes, I start to lower myself before him, keeping my gaze locked on his as I go to my knees. His breath hitches when the tip of my tongue touches the taut skin just under his swollen head. I trace the tip, trail through the crease, and then down the underside to kiss and lick his balls. He moans and slides his hand into my hair, readying it to guide me, but I don't need guidance. I'll allow it, but I don't need it.

Licking my way back up his shaft, I close my mouth over it and take him until he hits the back of my throat, stopping there to suction my cheeks around him before I slide up and down, keeping the pressure steady for a few strokes. When I reach the top again, I relax my cheeks and close my fingers around his increasing thickness, letting my saliva run down his length, my hand beginning to twist as I resume sucking and pumping. "That feels so good." His fingers tighten in my hair but it's more reflex than an attempt to give me direction. "God, yes. If you keep doing that, I'm going to come in your mouth."

I look up at him and pull off long enough to say, "I want you to come in my mouth."

He moans when I sheath his cock between my cheeks

again. His hand presses against the back of my head but I'm already headed in that direction. When I reengage with the rhythm—my hand twisting and my mouth gliding up and down his wet dick—he rolls his head and groans on a long exhale. The sound is growl and gravel. He swells and pulses against my tongue. Engorged veins and stretched skin test the flexibility of my jaw and the patience of my gag reflex, but I keep going because he's so close. His hips thrust forward, matching my pace as he fucks my mouth for a few strokes before he explodes, spilling into my mouth, taking full advantage of the permission I've granted. I swallow it all, lick him clean, and smile up at him.

I'm glad he's not a keep-score kind of guy when it comes to orgasms because there is no part of me that minds receiving more than I give, but if feels really good to have given him that release.

He pulls me upright and kisses me, walking me backward to the bed. "Lie down and spread your legs so I can taste that pretty pussy." I sit, lie back, and scoot up the mattress. He crawls over me, bends my knees, and pushes them toward my ears until my hips lift.

Wick smiles appreciatively at the position he's put me in. "Damn, you're flexible. Hold your legs open for me." I reach under my thighs and pull my knees farther apart. "Yeah, that's a good girl."

My pussy juices at his praise, and I feel my arousal trickle from my opening. He catches it on his tongue and drags it back up to lick around the perimeter before entering me. The heat from his mouth has me gushing a new stream for him to lap up. "I've missed this sweet little snatch. You shouldn't keep it away for so long."

His shoulders tense, and the way his head moves as he eats me out is erotic. I feel shameless and . . . deserving. That's what's different with him. I always believed I deserved pleasure as much as a man, but he makes me feel like I specifically deserve the exact attention and praise he gives me, like this is simply the way it's meant to be. I watch him for a while longer, feeling every shift, every lick and thrust of his tongue. But when he moves forward and begins to suck on my clit, my eyes shut and my head becomes one with the pillow. I come for him. For me, I mean. Because of him, but for me.

His dick is hard again but he moves my hands to let my legs fall before he pushes it inside me. Grateful for the reprieve, my hip flexors release. I hadn't realized they were being overstretched but I can feel it now as the tension starts to subside.

Wick kisses my neck. "Yeah, there you go. Keep those gorgeous legs open wide so you can take all this hard dick like a good girl." His raspy breath tickles my ear. "What are you, baby?"

"Daddy's good girl." My fingernails dig into his shoulders.

"Tell me what you want."

"Fuck me, Daddy. Fill my tight pussy with your thick hard cock."

He's biting my earlobe and pinching my nipple and his dick is stretching me in the most delectable way. This is definitely what I needed tonight. "You want to be Daddy's good little whore and cream on every inch?"

"Yes. I want it all, Daddy."

He thrusts deeper, driving forward until his balls slap against my ass. The fullness is exquisite and I savor every second that he lingers there. His eyes monitor my reactions: lids hooded, lip bitten, pussy definitely reacting exactly the way he called it. "Tell me what you are now so I can come inside your hot creamy cunt."

"Daddy's good little whore."

His whole body convulses as his release mixes with mine. When the spasms stop, he collapses on me and bites my earlobe again, teasingly, and then he whispers through his heaving breath, "I love that daddy kink."

"I never had it before you."

He pushes himself up onto his elbows. "You always had the kink, sweetheart. You just didn't have the daddy until I came along."

"You are so arrogant."

"You are so beautiful."

"Just so we're clear, I don't have *daddy issues*."

"That's good. I respect a woman who can compartmentalize. Just so we're clear, I'm not looking to be anybody's father figure either. I just like a good girl in bed."

"No, I'm pretty sure you'd be okay with a woman playing that role outside of bed, too."

He twirls a section of my hair. "No. I might joke about it, but I like strong women. I think your independence is sexy as hell, and that makes it all the more sexy when you call me daddy. You're an amazing woman, and a very, very good girl."

Every fiber in my body says I should hate this, but they're saying it while they unravel beneath him. And he was right. There's never been a man before him I could've done this with, but there was no learning curve, no adjustment period. He stuck one finger in my latte and launched me straight into the *fuck-me-daddy* stratosphere.

He rolls off me onto his side and plays with my nipples. "Have you ever used clamps?"

My shoulders rise up and curve inward. "Oh, hell no. The thought of that makes my nipples want to invert."

"They're adjustable," he says. "We should go shopping."

"I am not shopping for nipple clamps with you."

"Fine. I'll pick them out on my own."

"Let me say it another way. You're not using clamps on me."

"Pretty sure you'd enjoy them. And I haven't been wrong about you yet."

"Again, the arrogance."

"Again, the denial."

"How do you feel about brunch?"

"Are you offering to cook for me again?"

"I'm inviting you to join me and my friends for brunch in the morning."

"Seeking second opinions on me, huh?"

"Can you blame me?"

"Not at all. Sweet dreams." He kisses my forehead and rolls over.

I didn't get an answer about brunch. Maybe he needs to sleep on it? On my way to the bathroom, I see the blinking light on my phone so I grab it and take it with me.

Heath: *Finally got all the stickers off and you need to repaint my front door.*

Me: *Eat a bag of whale dicks.*

Heath: *You're so immature.*

Me: *Yeah, it's a real problem in my life.*

Heath: *I was serious about the door.*

Me: *I was serious about the whale dicks.*

Wick turns to face me when I get back into bed. "Yes, to brunch, by the way. But on one condition."

"What's that?"

"We go shopping afterwards."

SEVENTEEN
SAY MY NAME

O akley and Garth are seated next to each other when we arrive. The only person more skeptical than Oakley about a new man in a friend's life is Garth. They both have us captured in a lock-stare of judgment as we approach. I make the introductions, and we slide into the booth. Oakley and I are on the inside with Garth and Wick seated across from each other on the ends. I feel trapped already.

Wick went home to get ready this morning, and he smells like his bodywash, all sweet and charred. Garth is a connoisseur of scents with a highly sensitive nose. He will have an opinion.

Oakley has been analyzing his hands since the moment she laid eyes on him. She thinks you can tell a lot about a man from his hands. I agree, but we mean it for different reasons. For her, it's more about how steady they are and how often they're visible—does he rest them easily on the table or hide them in his lap—and a few other key factors. Her theories on the subject are detailed. And I guarantee the first think she did was check for a wedding band tan line, which isn't there. Like I would miss something that obvious.

I'm interested to see how Wick interacts with Garth. There's a lot to be learned about a straight man by the way he reacts to a gay man, especially a gay man who's covered in slithering snake tattoos, and who's currently wearing a reproduction of a vintage Queen concert tee, silver and turquoise drop earrings, and a handmade leather fedora that's both weathered and feathered. This is brunch casual for Garth. And as usual, he's rocking the whole ensemble, looking ready for a photoshoot.

Wick has no tattoos at all. And I'm pretty sure the only hat he's ever worn is a ballcap, and he's never owned anything with a feather in it unless it was a pillow. In fact, he's the most clean-cut, mainstream guy I've ever gone out with. Short hair, no tats, no piercings: the whole wholesome package. So not my type. Hell, even Hollis has tattoos and facial hair.

"What got you interested in becoming a personal trainer?" Garth asks, pulling a skewered jumbo shrimp from his bloody mary.

"When I left baseball, I needed an option that wouldn't trap me in an office. Started working on my certification, got a job in a gym, thinking the whole time it was something temporary I could do while I figured out my next step. And then I bought a condo I could renovate and rent out. Told myself maybe I'd go into real estate. But I took on a few private training clients, and then a few more, and then I bought another rental property, and next thing I knew, two part-time gigs became a full-time deal."

I didn't know he owned rental properties. That's why he was curious about my duplex. I wonder if he has any tenants who are ex-girlfriends. Not that it's any of my business.

"Baseball?" Garth perks up. How could I have forgotten what a huge baseball fan he is. We've only been to a million Astros games with him. "Who'd you play for?"

Wick rattles off the names of a couple minor league teams

that mean nothing to me but Garth knows exactly who they are. Of course, he does. He's a walking stats computer for all things baseball. My brain has blanked on a lot lately, but this, I should've been able to predict. He has a lot more in common with Wick than I do.

I order a mimosa and Wick gets a beer. We both go for the chicken and waffles. Okay, so we have some things in common outside of sex.

Oakley fills me in on her worst clients of the week and I tell her about the jackasses I encountered during my sales calls. Garth interrupts every now and then to offer his two cents on our terrible clients, because he can carry on two conversations at once. It's a skill. He's got baseball on the left and princesses and chauvinists on the right and I'm stuck in the middle in awe with Wick's heavy hand on my thigh, and Oakley's sparkling gaze noting his every move.

When the check arrives, Wick insists on picking up the tab, says it's the least he can do for crashing our brunch. As if he wasn't invited. The waiter walks away with his credit card, and Wick excuses himself to go to the bathroom.

"So, where are y'all going when we leave here?" Oakley asks, totally fishing to see if I'm spending the day with Wick. She could just come right out and ask, but it's more fun for her this way.

"I'm taking my car to have it detailed," Garth says. "One weekend at the beach and you have to vacuum your floormats for the rest of your life. Sand is Mother Nature's glitter. But it's all grit and no glam."

"I think we're going shopping," I say.

Garth leans forward. "Shopping for what?"

"Apparently, nipple clamps . . . " I look away and trail off to a near whisper when I say it.

Oakley and Garth look at each other, nod, and say in unison, "We like him."

"Because he wants to buy me nip clips?" Whoa, I definitely did not whisper that.

"Honey," Garth begins, "that man is exactly what you need right now. He can take your mind off your troubles and get you out of your comfort zone. That's a winning combination."

Oakley points to her left and says, "Yeah, what he said."

"He's not even my type, though."

"That makes it even better, girl," Garth adds with a grin. "Although, I think he might be exactly your type."

"Based on what?"

"Oh, I don't know," Oakley says. "Maybe the fact that if you'd scooted any closer to him, you'd have been in his lap."

"The way you giggle at every joke he makes," Garth says.

"And bite your lip whenever he does whatever he's been doing with his hand under the table." Oakley bites her lip to imitate what she claims I did.

"Okay, y'all can both calm down. He just had his hand on my thigh. I did not bite my lip. And I don't giggle." I widen my eyes to convey he's coming back to the table and this conversation is over.

The waiter returns his card with the receipts as soon as Wick sits down. "Here you go, Mr. Wickersham. Thank you all for coming in and I hope you enjoy the rest of your day."

"Thanks," Wick says, brushing his card aside to sign for the transaction.

"Your last name is Wickersham? Your name is Wick Wickersham?"

"Yeah, that's definitely my real name." He puts his card back in his wallet, and stares at me incredulously, like he's not even going to give me the satisfaction of laughing at the dumb joke I just made. His expression changes when he realizes I was serious, but the shock is still evident. "Wick is a shortened version of my last name. Something commonly referred to as a nickname, perhaps you've heard of them?"

"What's your real name?"

"Parker."

"Your name is Parker Wickersham? That's such a politician name."

Garth clears his throat. "Did you seriously not know his name until just now?"

"I knew his name," I say. "Just not his whole name."

Oakley laughs behind her hand, and averts her eyes. She's suddenly super interested in the assortment of sweetener packets between the salt and pepper shakers.

I know Wick has that cocky smile on his face before I even look at him again. "I don't know what to call you now."

"You know exactly what to call me." He says it in his deep dominant voice and his eyes rake over my body as the words leave his mouth. My cheeks flush. That did not just happen. "Unless you prefer Mr. President, since I'm such a politician." He knits his eyebrows together like he's giving it careful consideration. "Yeah, I might like that."

Garth fans himself. "Whew. I don't think I'm old enough for this show." He stands. "It was a pleasure to meet you, Mr. President. Thank you for brunch."

Oakley slides out of the booth. "It was nice to finally meet you, Wick. Thanks for brunch." She scurries to catch up to Garth and I have no doubt they're about to have a massive cackle-fest in the parking lot.

"What is wrong with you?"

Wick feigns shock. "What did I do?"

"You know what you did."

He kisses my forehead. "Come on, beautiful. Let's go shopping."

I have not had nearly enough champagne to be in an adult novelty shop in the middle of a Sunday afternoon. But I've apparently had just enough to softly sing along to "Unholy" while I stare at a glow-in-the-dark dildo, trying to figure out why someone would need that particular feature. It's very realistic looking, aside from the yellow-green shade of all things glow-in-the-dark. Right above it is multi-colored and swirled option meant to resemble a unicorn horn. The slogan on the package says "Twist the Rainbow," and in my head, I say it just like the old Skittles commercial.

I've only shopped for sex toys online. This place has some fascinating stuff. I look up to see Wick standing at the end of the aisle, watching me. He curls his finger in the *come here* motion and I know exactly what he wants to look at. An overhead sign near the back of the store catches my eye. "Machines," I say, reading it out loud. "What kind of machines?" I ask, looking to him for the answer.

Wick shakes his head at me and mouths "no."

I walk up to him and whisper, "I bet you're curious."

He laughs and says, "The things I'm curious about are this way." Taking my hand, he pulls me in the opposite direction.

There is a whole section of nipple clamp choices. "It would help if they had these things labeled by degree of torment," I say. "Where are the beginner models?"

Wick holds up a pair that are connected by a chain with spikes hanging from it.

"Um, no. That looks like some pro-level pain right there."

A woman comes around the corner and smiles at us. Her hot-pink shirt has the red-lipped logo of the store on it. She points to a pair that have no chains or dangling charms. "These are the best for beginners. They're lightweight and easy to adjust."

I lift the package from the display to check the weight. She's right. They're light. "How do you take them off?" I ask. "Do you have to unscrew them?"

"No, the screws are just to adjust the tension. You squeeze

to operate them." She pinches them through the bag to show me how easily they open.

"Oh, okay. Now I get it."

"These are cute." I turn to see Wick holding up a pair with big filigree butterfly charms hanging from short chains.

"Those are heavy," the woman says. "If you want something more decorative, I'd recommend these." She shows us a pair with feathery poms instead. They almost look like earrings.

"I like those," I say. "They look less clinical than the plain ones, and less painful than the butterflies."

"They're a good choice," she says. "There's a few colors to choose from." She gestures vaguely and then disappears around the corner, leaving us to make the final decision.

"Black?" I ask.

"If that's what you want."

"It's not my wants that brought us in here." I exchange the pair in my hands for ones with the black feathers.

"I know." He steps closer, and whispers, "But a deal's a deal."

"Even if we buy these, it doesn't mean I'm ever going to wear them."

He laughs. "Yeah, I know that, too. It's still hot that you're standing here, holding that package right now."

"Whatever you say, Parker."

"That doesn't bother me. You can use my first name if you want."

Well, way to take all the fun out of it.

Back in his car, he looks at me and says, "I really don't mind if you call me Parker. I honestly thought you knew that was my name."

I look at him and try to think of him as a Parker. Nope.

"I've known you as Wick for too long. I mean, not *known* you, obviously, but known who you were. You'll just always be Wick to me."

"Not always." He lowers his voice, raises his eyebrows.

"Yeah, could we keep that between us from now on?"

"I'm sorry. That came out of my mouth at brunch before I could stop myself, like a reflex."

"Ohhhhh," I say. "You have a daddy reflex. Yeah, that's totally not a thing."

"Oh, it's a thing. Trust me. And you trigger it like no woman I've ever known."

You trigger a few reflexes in me, too, Parker Wickersham. Wick. Daddy. Oof.

He reaches around to set the bag holding the nip clamps into the backseat.

"I have a hard time believing I'm the first woman who's ever called you daddy."

"I didn't say that. What I said was I never wanted it more than I do with you." The Jeep rolls to a stop at the edge of the lot. "Your friends are great, by the way."

"Oh, they thought you were hilarious."

"Because they knew I was teasing you. But I really won't do it again, okay? Just between us from now on. I promise."

"Thanks."

"Thanks who?"

"Wrong place, wrong time, Parker." Maybe I will want to call him by his first name sometimes. "What's your middle name?"

"Nathaniel."

"Oh, just stick a campaign sign in my yard already!"

"Was that a euphemism?"

"You wish."

"When it comes to you, beautiful, I have a very long list of wishes."

I point at the windshield. "You can go now."

He navigates us safely onto the road. Sometimes, I'm a bad passenger. I get uptight and don't trust that the person driving is watching and doing everything they should. I'd much rather drive than be driven, but I'm okay with Wick behind the wheel. I'm usually good with Oakley, but I'll always offer to drive, anyway. Jayce, I trusted, but not many before him. With Heath, I'd have felt safer roller skating down the middle of the freeway than riding in his passenger seat. So many clues I ignored. On a core level, I never really trusted him. I went into business with someone I didn't trust.

Growing up, people always told me I had good instincts. In college, my favorite professor said I couldn't help but be successful with such a sharp mind and keen instincts. What the hell happened to me? How did those instincts fail me so spectacularly?

Wick turns down the music. "Hey, you, distracted woman in my passenger seat. Did you hear me?"

"No, I'm sorry. Deep thoughts. What'd you say?"

"I asked what Heath did that made y'all break up. It's not really my business, I know, but ever since you said it was something worse than cheating, I can't stop wondering what it was."

"Oh. Yeah, I did say that, didn't I?" I take a deep breath. "He took some money out of our business accounts."

"Took? As in, stole?"

I can admit it to myself far easier than saying it to him. "Yeah, pretty much. I had to cover payroll from my personal savings, and replenish most of what he took from our operating account, too."

"He put it into that supplement company, didn't he?"

"Yep."

"He stole from you. You're busting your ass and he's out there acting like he's throwing around Monopoly money?"

"The sad thing is he genuinely believes it's a good investment. It's like he's been brainwashed."

"Because he has. But fuck that. It's not an excuse. Are you going after him for embezzlement?"

"I'm talking to an attorney." I leave it at that.

"Good. He probably won't try to work with me again since I didn't buy in, but if he does? No way. But I'll work with you for as long as you want. When his current package is up, don't worry about it. We're good."

"No, I don't want charity, least of all from you. I can pay you for sessions. I should be doing that, anyway, so it's all kosher with the gym. It's not right that I scan my regular membership card and then get a personal training session. As soon as you told me you couldn't transfer his sessions to me, I should've done it the right way. You could get in trouble and I didn't even think about it. That was selfish of me."

"I think it's pretty obvious I didn't mind seeing you instead of Heath. Nobody's going to get in trouble. Don't worry about it. Just keep showing up for your sessions."

"They're not my sessions until I have a training package in my name."

"You'll have one after tomorrow morning."

"After I buy one."

"You don't need to do that."

"Stop. You think you're being nice, that you're helping, but you're not. This whole situation with Heath makes me feel like a complete idiot. I already feel weak and spineless because I haven't taken certain actions that some people think I should. It's hard, okay? Everything is hard right now, but you paying for something behind my back is the worst possible thing you could do. Do not treat me like that."

"I get that things are hard. And I want to make them easier for you. In some small way, just let me help. Working out is good for stress. It's good for your health."

"Letting you be nice to me has boundaries. I still deserve to have my boundaries respected, Wick. And I have very strict financial boundaries. They've been violated in a major way but having someone else violate them in a smaller way won't help."

"I love your independence, but the stubbornness that comes with it is going to make me crazy."

"And I love your good intentions, but the need to be the big alpha protector who gets to rescue the damsel in distress is going to make me stop seeing you. As a trainer and as anything more."

"I don't have any desire to do that. I told you before, I like strong women."

"Mm-hmm, you like some things about us. But you can't handle the rest."

"I can handle anything you throw my way."

"All you need to do is listen to what I'm saying, Wick."

"He needs his ass kicked."

"Don't worry about that. I kicked his ass pretty good a few nights ago."

"*You* kicked his ass?"

"Basically."

"Walk me through that."

"It was more of a psychological ass kicking, okay, but it was pretty damn good, especially when he called me a bitch and I owned that shit and danced it out in front of his neighbors and—"

"When he called you a *what*?"

"If you're not going to let me talk then—"

"There is no such thing as a psychological ass kicking."

"Yes, there is."

"No, there's not. Did you psychologically break his jaw? Was he bleeding when you left?"

"His ego was."

Wick white-knuckles the steering wheel and I swear there's practically steam coming out of his nostrils, like a bull ready to charge. "I stand by my original claim. He needs his ass kicked."

I watch buildings whiz by through the window, and wish I'd never told him about the money. He doesn't pull onto the driveway when he gets to my place, just idles at the curb. "You'll be on my schedule for tomorrow morning. Don't stand me up, okay?" His smile is half-hearted, but his eyes are on fire, and not for me.

"Leave it alone, Wick. I mean it. It's my life and I've got it handled."

"Oh, I know. I'm sure he's still limping from that metaphorical ass kicking."

"Psychological. Don't be a prick. Why don't you come in for a while?"

"We've both got to be up early in the morning."

"If you were here, you could make sure I didn't skip that ridiculously early training session." I lean in to kiss him. He kisses me back but his whole body is stiff. "I really think all this powerful energy you're projecting right now could be put to better use."

"Oh, yeah? Convince me."

I trace the shell of his ear with my tongue and whisper, "You're going to make me beg? Please, Daddy."

"Don't try to use your psychological warfare on me." His smile turns up to full wattage, but he doesn't kill the engine.

If he leaves right now, I'm positive he's going to do something stupid, and as much as I hate this caveman impulse to physically kick someone's ass, especially on my behalf, I like him too much to let him fall victim to his own base instincts. "Stay here. Work your anger out on me instead."

"That's not something I ever want to do."

Shit. Wrong direction.

"I meant I could help you re-channel it." I rub his arm.

He kisses me again. "You're tempting, as always, but I need a little space to think right now."

Space to think, my ass. Desperate times . . . I reach into the back seat and bring the bag between us. "Are you sure that's what you want? Because I thought maybe you'd want to break these in."

"You play dirty."

"Only for you, Daddy."

He cuts the engine. Mission accomplished. Or put into motion, anyway.

EIGHTEEN
PREDICTABLY UNPREDICTABLE

The feathered clamps bounce on the mattress next to us when I stop bouncing on Wick's dick and sit all the way down. "My quads are done. We have to roll over."

"Already? I've gotta work your legs harder." He squeezes my quads, smiles up at me, and then glances over at the not-earrings.

"I don't know if I'm ready for those yet."

His thumbs brush across my nipples. "I think you are."

I loosened them to the lowest tension as soon as I took them out of the package and washed them, but they still felt strong when I pinched them opened and closed.

"Give me your hand." He opens one of the clamps and attaches it to the fleshy spot between my thumb and forefinger. The grip's not as mean as I expected. "See? They're not too tight."

"That's also not my nipple."

He removes the clamp and pulls my hand to his mouth to suck where it was attached. I squirm on top of him. "Seems like a sensitive spot to me," he teases. "Breathe."

My eyes close. There's no way I can watch him put it on.

His pinches my nipple and pulls it gently. The feathers tickle my skin and I shudder. And then I feel the bite.

It's not as intense as I'd expected. I still can't look. He repeats the process on the other side. His hands fall to my exhausted thighs, and he rubs over my weak muscles. "God-damn, that's hot."

I flutter my eyes open to look at him, and steel myself before I look down. His hands move up to my hips and he says, "Now, we can roll over."

As soon as we're flipped, he kisses me—a slow, deep kiss that lasts and lasts, and I know he's trying to take my mind off the clamps but I don't think anything could accomplish that. They don't hurt, necessarily, but they're not comfortable. I kiss him and breathe in his scent for a few minutes more before he takes his mouth away and begins to kiss his way down my neck and my chest. He flicks his tongue across my nipple and I barely feel it. I'm almost numb. I know this is supposed to happen, and when the clamps release, there will be a height-ened sensitivity. He's given me a taste every time he's used his fingers to pinch me but I know this is going to be so much more. He plays with the feathers, brushing them over my nipple.

His cock lurches and I'm not sure he's going to be able to hold out, but he looks up from my nipples to make eye contact as his fingers find my clit. It's hard to focus on his touch there, to stop fixating on the clamps and my anxious anticipation of having them removed. He dips his head to circle his tongue around my nipple again, and then he kisses his way down my stomach to let his tongue replace his fingers on my clit.

My thighs tremble and my pussy quivers under his hot breath, and I know he won't miss the clues that I'm on the brink. He never does. Sucking my clit into his mouth, he draws me closer to the edge. And then he reaches up and releases the clamps without warning and sensation reignites in my nipples like struck matches catching fire. His fingers claim them and knead and twist. My back arches, and his face follows my hips upward, never losing contact with my clit, sucking harder as I gasp for air and come with an intensity that slices a thin line between pain and euphoria.

I fall back to the mattress, shaking like I have a fever breaking. Chilled and burning up at the same time. "Oh, my God. That was incredible."

He kisses his way back up my body, dragging the blanket with him to warm me. "You are incredible." With the blanket draped over his back to block the air from my damp skin, he pushes his cock back inside my soaked pussy and fucks me with long hard strokes. I'm his entirely right now. Neither of us needs space.

Lying next to each other, our bodies still recovering, he lifts his arm. "Come here." I slide over and rest my head on his chest. He holds me tightly against him. His heartbeat is loud in my ear but I hear him clearly. "Just keep letting me be nice to you."

"For how much longer?"

"Until I'm done."

"That's what you always say, but that's not a timeframe."

"I know." He exhales long and slow, inhales with a contented snore.

I slip out from under his arm and roll over. His body follows and his hand squeezes my butt. He kisses my shoulder. "I'm going to kick this pretty little ass at the gym in the morning. And it won't be psychological."

"So arrogant. You do know there's a whole hurricane named after me right now, right?"

"Shhh, no scary stories at bedtime."

Wick says he doesn't need to go home to get ready for the gym; he has clothes there. Of course he does. I pull my hair into a ponytail, begrudgingly put on workout clothes, and lace up my shoes. When we walk into the lobby, he heads for the lockers, and I head for the membership liaison on duty. He backtracks and steers me away from the front desk. "Nope. You agreed to let me take care of this."

"I did not agree to that."

"Keep arguing. I'll keep adding squats to your workout." He stops at the door closest to the circuit training equipment. "Start warming up. I'll be back in less than five minutes."

I see through the glass that there are two bikes available but I don't want to climb on either one of them. "You bark a lot of orders at me for someone who claims he's trying to be nice."

"I don't get paid to be nice in here. Hit the bikes."

"You don't get paid to be nice to me anywhere."

"And yet, I do it, anyway. That's the epitome of nice." He opens the door for me.

I roll my eyes and step past him.

As promised, he's back in less than five. And he kicks my ass.

I take a second voluntary ass kicking in the gym on Wednesday morning, but it's probably nothing compared to the way I'm going to feel after I leave my meeting with Marlise. I opt to shower at home after my workout because the water pressure at the gym is like being hydroblasted, and my nipples are still tender. Those clamps were on me for less than ten minutes but they left a lasting impression. That orgasm though. Damn. Ten out of ten, will be trying again.

Wick owns more than a couple rental condos like he indicated at brunch—four, to be exact, plus two beach houses—and they're all in Galveston so he's on the island for the next few days doing storm prep. He's canceled all his bookings because he doesn't use a management company. He does everything himself, which couldn't be more on brand for him. He's busy with training clients next week, so he won't have time to go back down there if things change suddenly. Hurricane Nadine is still only a category one but the storm is stalled, churning and potentially building, and at this point, I'm over the jokes about how unpredictable and devastating she's bound to be with a name like mine. Cousins and coworkers are all suddenly comedians.

It's misting when I leave for Marlise's, and pouring by the time I arrive. She has an actual office in a building with a parking garage and a covered walkway, but she mostly only uses it for new client consultations, or meeting with the ones she doesn't care for on a personal level. I'm honored she schedules me at her home office, but today, it means getting drenched on my way to her front door. She welcomes me in with a towel in hand. "Do you not own an umbrella?"

"I hate umbrellas." I take the towel and wipe my arms before I start wringing out my hair. "They're a pain to deal with. It's a struggle to close them when you get in the car, and you get wet anyway. If the wind blows, they turn inside out. More trouble than they're worth."

"Anti-umbrella. Got it." She turns to lead me down the hall. "Come on back. I just made a fresh pot of coffee."

She has a kitchenette in her home office, which seems like a clear sign she works too damn much, if you ask me—that and the fact that she makes fresh pots of coffee at two-thirty in the afternoon. I accept a cup. It's good. Strong.

"You've seen the number," she says. "Talk to me."

"It's not like the amount was a shock. Honestly, I'm not sure I can be shocked anymore. But I may be about to shock you."

I open my purse. Marlise watches me with a wary expression. Her confusion amplifies when I hand her the sticker I took from my console a few days ago, and tucked into my wallet for safekeeping. "What is this?"

"It's a QR code. You scan it with your phone."

"You don't say? Honey, I didn't just wake up from a twenty-year coma. I recognize the symbol. What does it reveal?"

"I think it's better experienced than explained."

"As a general rule, attorneys tend not to be big fans of surprises." She puts her glasses on and wakes up her phone. "And I like them less than most."

"Well, just when you think Heath is all out of surprises . . ." I point to the sticker.

Her gaze narrows to focus on her phone screen. I know the moment she's read the creatively-worded message in the pop-up because her eyes nearly pop right out of their sockets. She watches a bit longer, taking in details from the homepage of Heath's BOTS promo site, and then she drops her phone and pinches the bridge of her nose. "Where did you get this and how long have you had it?"

"Tori, our store manager, called me Thursday night. I went in and confiscated the entire box he'd left there. He told a new employee she needed to put them on all our cups."

"You've had this for a week and I'm just now learning about it?"

I shift in my seat. "A little less than a week. I took the whole box, though, and I used them in a way that made sure he couldn't bring them back into the store. Trust me, he got the message." I don't volunteer that I didn't technically use *all* the stickers. For the first time, it occurs to me he could've had more than one box. But it doesn't matter; Tori made sure all our employees know they're not allowed to add anything to any of our packaging unless she approves it. No matter who it comes from.

"Oh, you sent a message? Well, that's bound to have helped the situation. If I didn't have another meeting this

afternoon, I'd be pouring whiskey in my coffee right now."
She glances at her cup like she's considering it, regardless.
"Keep talking."

I leave out the part with my dance routine. Pretty sure
she'd find it about as fierce as Wick's interpretation of it. And
frankly, Marlise looks like she wants to kick somebody's ass
right now, too—but I think it might be mine.

"He could've put these anywhere, Nadine. They could be
all over town. That pop-up implies Skweez endorses that shit
he's out there pimping like it's the cure for cancer." She drops
her head and sighs.

"I know. We need to send him a cease-and-desist letter or
something to get that message removed from his website."

She looks up at me, and I swear she's aged ten years since
I got here. "I don't represent Skweez. I cannot take any legal
action on their behalf. But if this gets brought to the attention
of their legal department? This is too far gone. You need to
sell. We need to reach out to that other franchisee in town and
see how interested he really is. First, I'll reach out to Heath
and try to put the fear of God in him about taking that
verbiage off his site. If he thinks it will prevent a sale, or I can
get him to understand the legal trouble he could face, maybe
he'll be reasonable."

"I agree about Heath. But I'm still not ready to sell,
Marlise."

"When, Nadine? When he's completely bankrupted you?
When you're named in a lawsuit right alongside him? There
are times to dig in and fight like hell, and there are times to
cut your losses."

"It's not fair that—"

"Don't you dare. Don't you dare sit there as smart as you
are and fall prey to that victim mentality bullshit. You're
culpable in this, too. Sure, you had a full plate, a career and a
new business venture." Her voice softens as she goes. "And
sometimes things slip. They go wrong when we're not looking.

It happens. But you've seen it now. You can't look away and ignore it and hope for the best. He's unstable and unpredictable." She tosses the sticker up and lets it fall to her desk to punctuate the moment.

I bang my hands on the arm of my chair. "Fuck. Fuck. Fuuuuuuuuuuuuuuuck!"

"Scream it out. Slam your head against the desk if you need to. Go for a run, whatever works for you. Burn through it. Get your head straight and make a decision. But I think you need to be honest with yourself. Do you want to hang on to the store to maintain the business or your ego? Shame hurts, but pride will cut you just as quick. Same knife, different side of the blade."

"You sound like Brené Brown."

"Thank you."

"I need a few days. I'll let you know something by end of business Friday."

"Do me a favor and don't send any more messages?"

"Yeah."

Her phone buzzes as we're wrapping up our goodbyes at the front door. She shakes her head after she reads the notification. "Your namesake storm just became a category two. But she's still stationary. I've got a bad feeling about this one."

"Everybody keeps saying that, but it's so far out there. It could turn in any direction. It could do anything at this point."

NINETEEN

NEW COORDINATES

By Friday morning, every news outlet is blasting the message that Hurricane Nadine is on the move. The coordinates have barely changed but the predictions have the storm coming in south of Galveston. I'm convinced meteorologists are all in a group chat where they just throw out wild guesses, maybe spin a wheel or something, and then they all agree to say the same thing.

Oakley calls before I've had my first cup of coffee. "Hey, we're having a hurricane party tonight."

"They're saying the storm is not even headed for us."

"Right. That's what we're celebrating. We can call it an un-hurricane party if it makes you feel better. A non-hurricane party?"

"You know the predictions will change again. Probably more than once. I don't think a premature celebration is a good idea. It's like daring the storm to turn around and come at us."

"Fine. Call it a bon voyage party where we wish the storm well on its journey. Just come over. And bring Wick so Hollis can meet him."

"How many people are coming?"

"It's a small get-together."

"It went from party to get-together awfully quick. Are we the only two people invited? Is this just so y'all can cross-examine Wick?"

"No, I promise. Jonna and Pepper may swing by. A few of Hollis's old teammates. Some of our neighbors. Garth said he may even bring someone."

"Well, damn. You can't drop that info and think I'm not going to show up. He never brings a date to anything."

"It's probably going to be the event of the year, honestly. You can't miss it."

"By tonight, I could probably use a party."

"You okay? What's going on?"

I'm lucky to have a best friend I can tell absolutely anything. Yet, somehow, I've not told her about the QR codes or my door decorating and subsequent dance performance. To be fair, it's the kind of thing I'd normally share at brunch if our weeks had been too busy to keep her updated, but Wick was at brunch. I don't have time to go through it all now. Besides, I don't want to kill her celebratory mood. "Some new ridiculousness from Heath. I'll bring you up to speed tomorrow. I'll be there tonight, but we're not discussing the chaos of my life until after the party." And after my decision.

I know there's no way the bank is going to finance my dream of becoming a sole proprietor, and this isn't the sort of thing I can cobble together with open credit card balances. After waking up over and over again all night long thinking about it, I know what I'm about to do is my only option. Marlise would say don't do it. Oakley would lie down behind my car to keep me from going. But he responded to my email yesterday and agreed to meet with me, so I have to think that's worth something.

～

I'm never early to a business meeting, but never late enough to make a negative impression either. I can read people, tell if they're a stickler for someone being right on time, or if they're going to judge me as too desperate for the deal if I don't unapologetically arrive within a five-to-ten-minute sweet spot. Usually, I know these things. But right now, my hypotheses might be as dicey as the meteorologists'.

He walks into the restaurant three people ahead of me. I don't recognize him from the back, but when he turns to the side, I know it's him. We make eye contact, and he smiles. "It's a pleasure to meet you Ms. Garrison." He extends his hand.

I complete the handshake. "Please, call me Nadine."

"Deal. And you can call me Greg. Mr. Blackwell is my father." He laughs and I try not to cringe. I hate when men use that line. Women never say smarmy shit like that.

"Thanks for meeting with me, Greg."

A hostess leads us to a table. After we're seated, I continue. "I've been meaning to check out your store for a while, but I haven't managed to make it over there yet."

"I'm not even going to pretend I haven't made a few reconnaissance trips to your location over the last few weeks. Your CPA's call piqued my curiosity."

"I hope it was busy."

"Seems like it's always busy. I may have gently pried a little information out of a few of your employees. They all seem happy, by the way. Profitable store, productive employees . . . so, why do you want out?"

"Well, that's the thing. I don't want out of the store, just out of my partnership."

"And your partner?"

"He needs out, financially."

"I see. You're not looking to sell. You're looking for a new partner."

"In my store only. I've done my homework. I know you hold your existing location under a corporation. I'm open to forming an LLC, but I don't want to get ahead of myself. We can certainly let our attorneys hash out the details if it's something you're interested in. I just thought we should meet, get to know one another a bit."

"I'm glad you reached out."

We leave the prospect of becoming partners off the table for the rest of our time together. He's a true businessman, which is fine because I didn't come here looking for a friend. I make sure the waitress knows we'll be on separate tickets. I don't need him to invest in me, just my business.

By the time we leave, I'm ready to give Marlise my decision. I don't have a firm commitment from Greg, but I know he's interested. And I'm not ready to sell. Until he says no, I'm still in the juice game.

Wick is back home, and agitated that he may have done all that storm prep for nothing, but such is life where we live, especially when you own property on the island and you insist on handling everything yourself. I know he knows that, so I don't say it out loud. He just needs to vent, and I can listen.

"Does the thought of going to a party tonight make you want to break things or cheer you up?"

"Depends. Where's this party?"

"At Oakley's. I've mentioned she lives with Hollis Nyx, right?"

"A party at Hollis Nyx's house? Like, I could meet the man himself?"

"The man, the myth, the legend. Yes."

"Hell. Fucking. Yeah. That sounds like an excellent way to end this week."

"It does, doesn't it?"

It hits me that Marlise may be at the party. She's not just Hollis's lawyer. They're friends. I gave her my decision over the phone this afternoon, and confessed about the meeting I'd set up without seeking her input. There was much sighing, and I'm sure the bridge of her nose is bruised from all the additional pinching my news inspired, but before we hung up, she said I had balls bigger than Dallas. I know she meant it to be criticism as much as compliment, but I could hear the smile in her voice. She admires me at least a little. She might want to shake me for not telling her my plan, but she's in the game with me.

There are about a dozen people at the party when Wick and I walk in. This is good, not a huge crowd but not so small that Wick is spotlighted. Not that he couldn't handle a spotlight.

Oakley's bosses, Jonna and Pepper wave from across the room. They're the first ones I introduce to Wick. There aren't two women on the planet who are better at parties than Jonna and Pepper. They've built a whole business around them.

While Pepper has Wick engaged in conversation, Jonna gives me a discreet wink and a thumbs-up. I mouth back, "I know, right?" Because, yeah, he's hot.

We make our way into the kitchen to get drinks, and find Hollis opening a fresh bottle of wine. Knowing that Wick aimed for the pros but didn't make it had my stomach in knots on the way over. We haven't talked about it since that morning in his bedroom, but what if Hollis is a painful reminder of things Wick wanted but didn't achieve? The fame. The legacy. This house!

But no, they hit it off like they've known each other their whole lives. I know Wick is a huge fan, but two minutes after they're introduced, they're just two dudes, talking sports in the kitchen at a party.

I wander off in search of Oakley and find her in the wine cellar, sticking sparklers in the top of an elaborately decorated chocolate cake. Garth is assisting. "Where's you date?" I ask him.

"I reconsidered. He's shy." He rearranges the last two sparklers Oakley has planted. "Between you two and Jonna and Pepper fawning all over him, he'd have had an anxiety attack."

"Why do you make us out to be like that? We would've been so chill with him."

"See, I know you believe those words as they're leaving your mouth but—"

"Shh," Oakley says. "Hollis isn't coming, is he?" She eyes me like I have some sort of sixth sense when it comes to his approach.

"No, he's in the kitchen with Wick. What are y'all doing in here?"

"He busted me planning that surprise party for his fortieth birthday, and he made me promise to stop. But tonight's party was totally his idea. When I went to buy food for it, I saw the cakes in the bakery, and the perfect plan came together. So, now we're having a hurricane party with a birthday cake."

"You're hijacking his hurricane party and turning it into his surprise birthday party? Two months early?"

"Kinda guarantees it'll be a surprise, doesn't it?"

Garth shrugs and makes a face that says *Don't look at me. I'm just doing what she asked.*

"Never let it be said you're not resourceful."

"Never let it be said I got cheated out of planning a party!"

Hollis is not going to love this, but he'll accept that she found a way to do exactly what she wanted. Honestly, he should've seen it coming. "That cake looks amazing."

"It's about to look even more amazing." Oakley holds up a lighter. "You carry it," she tells Garth. "Stop at the end of the hallway and I'll light it up right before we take it into the kitchen."

She turns to me. "You go ahead of us and quietly direct everybody toward the kitchen. We'll give you a few minutes. Just be cool about it. Don't let Hollis get suspicious."

"What could possibly tip him off?"

Directing people to the kitchen is the easy part. Preventing Hollis from noticing the guests are swarming is a complete impossibility. He catches my eyes and all I can do is mouth, "I'm sorry. Happy birthday."

Oakley, Garth and the sparkling cake make their entrance, and she starts to sing. To his credit, Hollis laughs. *And the award for good sportsmanship goes to . . . Hollis Nyx!*

My scheming best friend beams as Garth sets the cake on the island. She is so pleased with herself right now.

Wick helps me open and pour champagne. Flutes are passed around the room, and for a little while longer, no one will worry about tracking a storm or saving a business or kicking anyone's ass . . . we will eat cake and be happy to be at the party, whatever the occasion.

TWENTY
POOLSIDE CONFESSIONS

I wake up next to Wick in a guest room. We stayed to help clean up after the party, and then we just stayed. But he has clients this morning and I know his alarm will go off soon. He opens his eyes and catches me watching him. "Stop being creepy." He lifts his arm and I slide into my favorite spot.

I'm almost back asleep when his alarm starts. "Nooooo, make it stop," I whine. He shuts it off, but then he slips out of bed and leaves me with no warm body to hold. I need to get up to lock the door behind him, anyway. Oakley's taking me home later but I doubt if she and Hollis are up yet.

I head straight for the kitchen to make coffee after I say goodbye to Wick. There's cake leftover because some people refused a slice last night. Fools. This cake is delicious. Perfect breakfast.

Hollis is lured out of bed by the smell of coffee, and finds me leaning against the counter, forking another bite of cake from the box. "You know you can cut yourself a whole slice, right? We have these amazing tools called knives."

"It tastes better this way. Plus, I don't have to wash a plate."

He pours himself a cup of coffee, and lifts a fork from the drawer. "Sometimes, you think like a teenager."

"More often than you want to know."

"Don't tell Oakley," he says, sticking his fork into the remaining wedge of cake.

"Don't tell me what?" She stumbles into view and yawns. "Oh, my God. Heathens." Hollis opens the drawer for her. She takes a fork and joins us for breakfast.

He eats a few more bites before he kisses Oakley on the head, and disappears down the hall to take a shower. He's spending his day at Nyx International. Even the morning after his non-hurricane, not-birthday party, he's a workaholic.

Oakley grabs a mug and the coffee pot. "Bring the cake," she says. I follow her out the back door. Their pool looks inviting, dazzled by the glitz of early morning sunlight. We sit under a covered section of the patio and polish off the cake. "What's happening with Heath?" she says after insisting I eat the last bite.

I top off my coffee and start with the phone call from Tori, giving her the full play-by-play, right through my phone call with Marlise yesterday afternoon.

She laughs when I repeat Marlise's comment about my balls. "Hollis says that about you all the time."

"I'm flattered."

"You should be. It's not like he compliments every woman's balls. How have you not told me any of this?"

"It sounds crazy but there hasn't really been time."

"There is always time to tell me important stuff about your life! If Greg buys out Heath, you'll have a new business partner you've known for even less time than you knew the last one."

"Yeah, but at least this one's an actual businessman. Heath goes around saying he is, but he's just gotten lucky with a few good investments. And now, he's drowning in the worst investment ever. He doesn't know how to run a business. He wants to sink some money in, cash out, and move on. Taking a buyout should be perfect for him. It's probably how he envisioned this ending all along."

"True. He's going to lose every dime."

"Probably. But at least they'll be his own dimes."

"I do like the thought of him being completely out of your life."

"This is the only way I can see that happening without having to sell the store. Cross your fingers for me."

"My fingers and my toes. You want to hang out and have a pool day?"

"I thought you had errands to run."

"I'll do them tomorrow."

"If you don't want your husband to see me naked in your pool, you better go get me a bathing suit in the next two minutes."

"Did you just call him my husband?"

"Everyone calls him your husband. Every time he takes you on a trip, I expect you to come back married."

"Like I'd skip out on getting to plan my own wedding. Or forcing you to wear a yellow dress as my maid of honor."

"I think we both know I'm wearing black. Pants. A tux, probably."

"Why not shorts?"

"Well, damn. Now I have to pick out different shoes."

She goes inside to get me a suit. My therapist's office sends me an automated reminder about my appointment on Monday. I rescheduled last week, but I think I'll make time for this one. It's hard to reconcile the way therapy drags me through the past time and time again while the world around me is constantly broadcasting the advice to live in the moment, seize the day, and never look back . . . but I do understand that there's a difference between moving on from the past and hiding from it. I still grapple with a lot of things, question if therapy is a means to growth or a crutch. I've grown during it; I just don't know if I've grown because of it, or if I would've changed anyway. I guess maybe that's one of the reasons I keep going, to answer that question about myself. That and the fact that I've always been motivated by accountability. I go to confess.

Oakley opens the back door, and says, "Are you coming in to put this on or do you plan to change in the bushes?"

Lying in the sun with drops of pool water on my skin, it feels like if I don't tell Oakley now, I never will. I take a breath and say it before I change my mind. "I checked in on Jayce not long ago."

"Called him or quietly stalked his pics?"

"I didn't call him. He's engaged. I was going to tell you that day at brunch, right before the call from Paula that blew up my life."

"Don't go down that road. Don't start thinking you made the wrong choice just because things are rough right now. Taking that job in Alaska was the right move for him, but you know what you felt when you went there."

"What if I decided too soon?"

"Jayce was never comfortable living in Houston. He was destined to go live off the grid with a yard full of bears, catching his dinner from a stream every night. And you would've never been happy there. You didn't want the same life he did."

"He lives in Anchorage. It's not exactly the wilderness you make it out to be."

"Y'all were growing apart, Nade. The end was coming, whether it happened in Houston or Anchorage. You said so yourself as soon as you came home."

"I know. It's just . . . he was probably the best guy I ever dated."

"Oh, he was absolutely the best guy you ever dated. But no matter how good he was, he would've never been good enough because he wasn't the one for you. You weren't the one for each other."

Tears roll down my cheeks. "Maybe I'm reminiscing about Jayce so much because that was the last time I felt this sad."

"You're beating yourself up right now, thinking all your choices have been bad, but that's not true. You've made a hell of a lot of good choices in your life, Nade. Wick seems like a pretty good choice."

"Yeah, but it feels an awful lot like things felt with Jayce at this point, and that's terrifying. How am I supposed to know if anything is a good choice before it blows up in my face? What if I'm not capable of recognizing red flags?"

"There were no red flags with Jayce. Your relationship didn't blow up. It just came to a natural end."

"What about the red flags with Heath?"

"Nobody could've predicted how things would turn out with Heath."

"I think Marlise might have."

"Yeah, well, Marlise is a superhero and we don't compare ourselves to her."

"She all but told me she saw it coming. She structured our partnership with the end in mind."

"Not all heroes wear capes, babe."

"Well, I'm wearing one to your wedding. With sequins. Shorts and a fully sequined cape."

"With thigh-high boots, please."

"Definitely. And this bikini top."

"Perfect. That's one less decision I have to make when the time comes."

"Me and my good decisions, on the job since the day I hit puberty."

"Can't wait to show my kids the photos of Aunt Nay Nay from my wedding."

"Oh, your kids are going to worship me."

"Without a doubt." She rolls over. "So, how bad did you

and your personal trainer wreck my sheets? Can they be washed or should I just burn them?"

"You might want to wash them twice."

We laugh as the sun beats down. I close my eyes and ignore the sting on my cheeks.

Come on, Greg Blackwell. See me as a good choice.

TWENTY-ONE
EASY BREEZY

By mid-week, I'm so anxious to hear from Greg, I jump every time my phone buzzes. Marlise texted first thing this morning to let me know Heath thinks he deserves a higher buyout. She tried to set him straight but feels sure I'll hear from him soon. I had to promise her I wouldn't let him get to me. I know my role: remain professional, do not argue, refer him back to her—and don't sign off with "fuck you, you fucking stupid-ass fuckwit," no matter how many insults or negative epithets he flings at me first. No retaliation. No interpretive dance moves. No defacing of property. Calm, cool, and collected until the end.

I have hereby solemnly sworn to comply with all her requests regarding my behavior. This sucks but I keep telling myself it'll be over soon. He hasn't made any more appearances at Skweez or touched the bank accounts. As long as that holds, I can uphold my promises to Marlise.

I'm blow drying my hair, getting ready to head to the office for a meeting that probably could've been an email, when the sight of my arm in the mirror shocks me. There's noticeable muscle tone there. I set the hair dryer down and lift the other arm to check it out. Nice. Turning to the side, I lift my towel and look at the pronounced curve of my ass. My butt cheeks are rounded and firm. Nobody is going to mistake me for J-Lo anytime soon, but these defined shapes are proof of my hard work in the gym. Wick has commented on it, but he always compliments me. I hadn't really seen it until just now. For the first time in weeks, I feel more satisfaction than disgust when I look at my reflection.

Heath waits until I'm in the car, rolling through rush-hour traffic, to call me. I should let it go to voicemail but I'm not that strong yet. "Hello."

"It's bad enough you turned our attorney against me, but now even our employees don't respect me."

"What are you doing at the store?"

"I just stopped in to see how things were going."

"And?"

"And I got ignored like I was nobody."

"Early mornings are hectic, Heath. You know that. They can't stop and entertain you. Why would you go in at a time like that?" My nerves are sizzling like a lit fuse. He better not have tried to pull another fast one. So help me . . .

"I. Am. Still. An. Owner. You can't prevent from going in there."

"I was simply inquiring about the purpose of your visit." *Breathe. Inhale. Exhale.* A horn blows behind me. The white Mercedes that blew it whips into the adjacent lane to pass me, nearly taking my bumper with him. "Fuck you, asshole!"

"Fuck you, Nadine!"

"No, no, no, no, I wasn't saying that to you. This impatient jerk just nearly clipped my bumper trying to get around me. I'm going eighty like everybody else, but he apparently needs to go a hundred."

"Damn, I can't believe traffic's moving that fast at this time of day."

"I know, right? He should feel lucky we're not all sitting still."

"Give it a few miles."

I laugh. "Exactly." *Shit. Are we having a normal conversation?* "I really don't think anybody at the store was trying to disrespect you. They were probably just slammed. It was busy, wasn't it?"

"Yeah, it was packed. You do realize I know how much money the store is bringing in, right?"

Okay, here it comes. "What are you trying to say?"

"You can't cheat me out of my fair share. It's not right."

"No one is attempting to cheat you out of anything. There is a formula for determining a buyout offer, Heath. I'm sure Marlise will be happy to go over our buy and sell agreement with you and show you exactly how it was calculated. It's not an arbitrary number." I bite my tongue before I point out that his repayment of my capital contribution being included is not only fair, it's required.

"I never agreed to those terms though."

"You did. We both did. It's part of our partnership agreement."

"How do you have that kind of money, anyway?"

Deep breaths. Don't say too much. "I don't know that I do yet. But we need to be on the same page before I secure funding."

"What if I don't agree? What if you can't get the money?"

"Then we have to sell."

"Why? The store is doing fine."

"Heath, your focus is not on Skweez. You want more money to invest in Bounty of the Seas, right? This would give you a lump-sum payment to do whatever you want with. I'm not asking you to accept a payment schedule."

"I would never agree to that."

"You really need to go over our buy and sell agreement. It's obvious you have no idea what you've already agreed to. Please reach out to Marlise for further clarification. I need to get off the phone."

"You're not putting me on any kind of payment plan, Nadine! I want all my money upfront."

"Traffic's backing up, Heath. I've gotta go." I end the call. He's told me everything I need to know. He'll take the money and run. He just wants his voice heard on the way out. *Bye-bye, baby venture capitalist. Don't get your swinging dick caught in a juicer on the way out.*

Hurricane Nadine is still hanging out in the Gulf, still gaining strength. Wick hasn't undone any of his storm prep or rebooked his beach rentals, just in case, but Galveston's safe at the moment, so we're island-bound on a Friday evening.

I mentioned I've always loved the beach when there's a storm in the Gulf, and the next thing I knew, he was at my door—only we weren't just going to dinner anymore, we were spending the weekend together in one of his beach houses.

If the current southbound-45 gridlock is any indication, the choppy surf and cloudy skies aren't keeping many people away.

I checked in with Marlise before we left. She interrupted me two minutes into the conversation and said, "Take your ass to the beach. Chill out for a few days. Nothing is going to change between now and Monday."

Everything is taking so long and I hate not knowing where things stand. I just want answers. Yesterday.

When we turn left onto Seawall and head for the west end, Wick rolls down our windows, and my body relaxes a little. The sun's going down, and the warm breeze blowing through the car smells the way all summer nights should: like saltwater kisses and things growing wild.

His house we're staying in is only two rows from the water. Prime real estate. When we walk inside, he hits a button to raise the electric storm shutters. I turn and check out the open-concept living, dining & kitchen space.

"Wow. This is really nice, Wick. Did it come decorated?" I

don't mean that to be offensive, but the house he lives in has a very minimalist aesthetic, and this place looks like it could be featured in a magazine.

For the first time ever, his grin looks sheepish. "I was dating an interior designer at the time."

"Nice. Do you still have her number?"

He laughs. "She moved out of state after we split up."

"Cool. I ran my ex out of the state, too."

"It's a skill not everybody has."

"Mine went all the way to Alaska."

"You win. Mine only went to Georgia."

"And you didn't go because you hate peaches?"

"I didn't go because it wasn't meant to be."

"Yeah, same here." *Freakishly same.*

"Why are you looking at me like that?"

"I'm just wondering what our age difference is. It can't be much, but you've got to be older than me to have played minor league baseball and own as many properties as you do. If you're not, I'm going to throw myself into the surf."

His eyes stay fixed on mine. "I'm thirty-three."

"I'm twenty-eight. Okay, so I've got five years to buy six properties."

"Playing minor league baseball is probably going to be a bigger hurdle."

"I own a juice bar. Can I get some points for that?" I wince as soon as I've said it, because I only half-own it, and even that's hanging in the balance.

He steps forward and rests his hands on my hips. "You don't need any points from me or anyone else. You're doing great."

"Yeah, at so many things."

"Should I make you a list?"

"I'm pretty sure I know everything that would be on your list."

"I might surprise you." His lips meet mine and I can taste

the salt on his skin. "Do you want to go for a walk on the beach?"

"Yes."

We hold hands and walk along the water's edge. I let myself get lost in that beach magic that makes it feel like you've known someone forever. A woman jogs by with her dog. We duck a wildly-thrown Frisbee, and laugh as the teenage boy who threw it runs to retrieve it, and yells a frantic apology. It's getting darker but the moon is nearly full. The water's rough, the way it always is when there's a storm offshore. Everything feels familiar, as if we do this every night. Beach magic.

When we get back to the house, we kick our shoes off at the door—another déjà vu moment. He opens a bottle of wine, and we sit on the upstairs deck off the main bedroom. We can hear the waves crash and see the moonlight flickering on the distant surface. "Why'd you quit playing baseball? Did you have to?"

"Technically, no, but realistically, my chances of getting called up were extremely low, and I could definitely make more money doing something else. I'd had two knee surgeries and just wasn't loving the life anymore."

"Were you sad?"

"More lost than sad. I had no fucking idea what I wanted to do. Nothing felt right. I was halfway through a degree when I got signed but I had zero desire to go back to school, just to end up stuck at a computer all day for the rest of my life."

"But you're happy now?"

"Yeah, I got lucky, I guess. Things worked out."

"You make it sound like the life you created fell into your lap, but I know it didn't."

"I never minded having to work. And I like a challenge, so when people said I couldn't make a living as a personal trainer, I didn't listen. When they said flipping real estate was too risky, I rushed right in. I had a little construction knowledge, and I figured I always learned best by doing, anyway. Then I stopped flipping and started keeping the properties I bought. And then I stopped adding new properties and kept managing the ones I owned, and here I am."

"Which do you like better, being a personal trainer, or the property management?"

"Both. I don't like doing the same thing all the time."

"I've noticed."

"You complaining?"

"Not even."

"What made you buy a juice bar?"

"You know, if I could go back in time and figure that one out, I would. It was just a gut feeling."

"That feels good, doesn't it? Trusting your gut?"

It's hard to remember. All I've been doing lately is second-guessing mine. Except for setting up the meeting with Greg Blackwell. And the results of that move are yet to be seen. "Yeah," I say. "It does."

"You don't sound sure."

"Did you ever just really want a particular property, but somebody else put in a better offer?"

"Uh, yeah. Multiple times."

"And you just let it go and moved on?"

"I can't force a seller to take my offer any more than they could force me to make one. Offers either get accepted or they don't. There's always another property."

"Right." He's so logical. The way I used to be. Why am I desperate to keep the juice bar? It's not my sole source of income. I'm not the founder of Skweez. I don't have some deep abiding passion for juice. If I sold it, I could always invest in something else. Fuck. Maybe I am letting my ego lead.

"But sometimes people think they can force you into things like that. I had a guy insist he was going to buy this place, even though it wasn't on the market. He was convinced I was going to sell him this house."

"Was he making a good offer?"

"Yeah, but I didn't need his money. This house makes me money, thanks to my risk and my sweat equity . . . it's mine. Nobody was going to bully me into selling it. Plus, I didn't like the guy, so fuck him."

"Thank you."

"For what?"

"Being human."

"As opposed to?"

"Something a little too perfect."

"You want imperfect? I've got imperfections for days." His hand fans down his body—over his broad chest and tight abs, falling away when it reaches his muscular legs. All that warmth and strength being showcased like I might possibly find something to fault.

"Are you ready to go to bed, Mr. Imperfect?"

"I am always ready to take you to bed, *kitten*." If it's possible to smirk a word, he just did. I give him the look, and he laughs. "I'm sorry. I forgot you hate that nickname."

"Oh, you forgot, huh?" I stand and turn to go inside, knowing he'll follow.

He closes the space between us as soon as we're in the bedroom. His chest presses against my back and his arms encircle my waist as he kisses my neck. "I could never forget anything about you. But I had to rile you up just a little. I like it when you're feisty at bedtime."

"Ahhhh, and there's that other word I don't like being called." I can't even pretend to be mad because he's playfully biting my neck and his arms have closed in tighter.

"But you're such a good little feisty kitten."

I wiggle and try to break free. He loosens his arms just enough to tickle my ribs, which makes me wiggle harder, trying to escape his fingers. "Oh, that's it. It's just you and your hand tonight, bud."

"Oh, yeah?" He drops his arms and I lunge forward, laughing. His eyes have that wicked glint. "I'm on my own, am I?"

"That's what I said." I sit on the end of the bed and look at him, standing there in all his arrogant glory.

He pulls his shirt off, swings it around in front of him a few times before tossing it at my face. I catch it, and fling it aside like I'm entirely unimpressed. His cocky smile lets me know he thoroughly believes there's going to be a team effort unfolding soon. He unbuttons his shorts and teases his zipper up and down a few inches. I bite the inside of my lip to keep from laughing. He's so ridiculous.

When he drags the toggle all the way down and takes out his hard cock, the urge to laugh dissipates, but my teeth continue to sink into my flesh. *Damn, that initial view still gets me every time.*

His hand wraps around his erection and I can't peel my eyes off it. My own hand recalls the feel of it, such soft skin over a dick so hard. I cross my legs and kick my foot as if I'm growing bored with the show, but the truth is my clit is already crying for a little friction.

"If I've gotta take care of me, you're on your own too, sweetheart."

"That's cool. I can take care of me just fine."

"I should get to watch you, too, then. It's only fair."

"Okay." I go up onto my knees to remove my shirt and bra, sit back down to shimmy out of my shorts and under-wear. "I didn't realize you were in a hurry," I say.

"Are you claiming you can outlast me?"

"Are you proposing a challenge?" I slide up on the mattress and pull two pillows down to prop my shoulders and head before I lie back.

"My favorite way to do anything," he says. "But you need

more pillows. We have to be able to keep our eyes on each other."

I slide closer to the headboard so I can lean against it, and add the other two pillows to my stack so my whole upper body is cushioned. This setup gives me a clear view of him standing at the foot of the bed with pre-cum leaking onto the swollen head burgeoning from his grip.

He groans when my thighs part and my hips slide into position. The only light is from the one bedside lamp I turned on when we came upstairs. It creates a glow similar to being on the beach under only the moonlight. The sliding door that leads outside is still open, and the fury of the crashing waves is our soundtrack.

I spread myself open to tease him. "Stroke it," he commands. "Winner comes first, not last."

"A game you can't lose. Cheater. What's the prize this time?"

"Same as before. Winner gets to choose, loser can't refuse."

"I've been letting you be nice to me for weeks now."

"Maybe I'm ready to be something other than nice."

Holy shit. That comment rolled off his tongue with a vibration that licked right through my dripping pussy. I might win this thing after all. Two fingers glide through my juices, circling my clit a few times before I slip them inside and fuck myself while he jacks his cock. My thumb traces the perimeter of my clit, and it swells under the pressure.

He jerks himself so much rougher than I ever could. It looks like it should hurt but he doesn't let up. I want him to be rough with me instead, to let my walls squeeze him instead of his hand.

My hips rock up and back like they would if I were rising to meet his thrusts. I so want to feel him mercilessly slamming into me, the fleeting pain of him forcing me to take all of him in one long stroke, and then the incredible full, pulling sensation when he withdraws before he drives it back in. My clit's too sensitive for the pressure I'm inflicting. I lighten my touch but Wick's body is already starting to tense. He's way ahead of me. The only way I could win would be to do or say something to ruin it for him, but I'd never.

He is way too sexy when he combusts into a raging orgasm, exactly the way he is right now with bursts erupting in thick jets all over his hand. My hand stills as I watch the last spurt leave him. The intense sear of his stare goes straight to my fingers, resting on my pussy. "Did I tell you to stop?"

"You won."

"Finish."

"Finish me."

For a split-second, I think I've spoiled the moment, that he's angry and about to walk away. But he lifts his knee to climb onto the bed between my legs. "Say please."

"Please, daddy."

His open mouth crashes against my pussy, his teeth grazing my delicate skin, his tongue tasting me, inside and out. This isn't the roughness I was thinking about before, but there is nothing gentle about it. He doesn't half-do anything. I fist the comforter when he starts to tease my clit, and let him pull me across the finish line, coming all over his face like this moment should have been preceded with a disclaimer and a souvenir raincoat.

While I'm still recovering, he looks up with a sheen and a smile on his face.

"I thought you said you were done being nice to me," I say.

"No, I said I was ready to be something else in addition to, not instead of. Roll over."

Once again, my body responds to his command prematurely, before my brain can give it due consideration. When his hand slaps my ass, I realize my body knew what it was doing all along. He's never spanked me before. I assumed he wasn't into it, despite our flirty jokes that first day in his hot tub, but I guess he just prefers to take things in stages.

He delivers another slap and the stinging sensation that remains after he lifts his hand renders me tense with anticipation of the next one. And the one after that, however many it takes for pain to become pleasure. I need him to take me to that space, to get me truly out of my head, but before this moment, I hadn't thought it mattered whether he ever took me there or not. He's introduced me to new things, but having him do this old thing might leave a more lasting impression than just his handprint. *Not instead of, but in addition to . . .*

When I begin to retreat from his spanking, he pulls me back and rubs my inflamed cheeks, soothing the burning sensation on my skin. "I've wanted to make this pretty little ass glow since the first time I saw it."

"Why'd you wait?"

"Because timing matters." He slips his middle finger between my cheeks, dips it down until it's coated in my arousal, and then teases it around the opening he's not yet tried. "And some things are better when you don't rush."

Oof. If this was a preview for a movie, I'd be yelling "take my money!" right now. But it's not a movie. It's my real life, and he's stealing the show.

He slips his finger halfway inside, and my breath catches. "I didn't pack lube."

"Would you have brought some if I'd asked?" His finger goes deeper. "Or been okay if I'd brought it?"

I understand the depth of the question. "I'm not entirely opposed to anal, but I'm not sure how I'd have felt about it tonight."

"Another time."

"Yeah."

"No rush." He gives me his trademark grin, but it seems less cocky, more intimate and enticing. "We should shower."

"You should probably take your finger out of my ass first."

TWENTY-TWO
THE DIRTY SIDE

Saturday morning brings sunnier skies and news that Hurricane Nadine is moving. Predictions are trending even farther south on the Texas coast. We're having breakfast in a place full of locals so we've gotten up-to-the-minute updates.

I'm sorry for whatever area ultimately has to bear the brunt of the storm, but I'm glad it looks like it won't be close enough to cause any major problems in Houston. It always feels terrible to be grateful someone else is getting a hurricane instead of us, but our turn will come back around.

Wick's considering reopening availability for his properties but he has the rest of today to decide. We're not going home until tomorrow afternoon. "I knew this hurricane wasn't going to hit here," I say.

"Don't get too confident."

"I'm always confident about a fellow Nadine."

He steals a slice of bacon from my plate. "It's still a big storm, and we're still on the dirty side."

"Hmm, I guess that puts you on the dirty side of two Nadines."

"You don't have a clean side."

I toss a blueberry at him. He catches it in his mouth. "Good reflexes."

"It's almost like I used to have a job where catching round objects was important."

"You didn't catch baseballs in your mouth."

"Only a few."

After breakfast, we plant chairs in the sand and watch birds and waves, and talk about nothing that matters in between long stretches of comfortable silence. We're not alone on the beach but it's not crowded. A dog barks at the waves. Another tries to catch seagulls. A trio of little kids builds sandcastles a few yards away, while their moms sit on overlapping beach towels and gossip too loudly about other moms, who are probably all together somewhere else, gossiping about them. One of the kids throws a shovel when they have to leave, one cries, and the other's a little suck-ass who repeatedly points out how she's the only one being good so she deserves a treat but the other two kids shouldn't get one.

Wick rolls his head toward me and says, "Middle school is going to be rough for that one."

"And her mommy."

I like that his laugh comes easily, and the way the smile remains on his face. His eyes are hidden by sunglasses but I don't have to see them to know they're the color of yesterday's sky, yet bright like today's. There's a heaviness to all of him, but lightness, too. Serious, but always ready with a witty come-back. Domineering to a degree, but kind.

We pack up not long after the pre-k tantrums have cleared out.

A yawn overtakes me as I kick my shoes off inside the door. "How can a day spent doing nothing be so exhausting?"

"You don't know the difference between being exhausted and being relaxed, which tells me you don't relax nearly enough."

"And you do? With all your clients and properties, splitting your time between Houston and here?"

"When I'm here to work, I work. When I'm here to relax, I relax."

"It's just that easy, huh? Like flipping a switch."

"Things are usually as easy or as hard as we make them."

"Some things are just hard, no matter what."

"A few. But most? Our attitude heavily influences the outcome."

"Okay, Zen master."

"What I said was the opposite of Zen. I'm saying conscious effort makes the difference."

"Are you going to argue with everything I say today?"

"Are you going to agree with anything I say?"

"Oil and water."

"Fire and ice."

"We should probably just turn and walk away from each other right now." I shrug and sigh dramatically.

He walks toward me with a fiery glow in his eyes. "Or we could meet in the middle."

My hands rest on his chest when his arms encircle my waist, as if I might push him away. As if I could. "What's at the middle of fire and ice?"

"Hot water," he says, his voice deepening. "Which is where this whole thing started."

"If only you had a hot tub here."

"I have a bathtub big enough for two. We could shower off and soak for a while."

"Until you convince me I'm relaxed?"

"Or I show you how it really feels to have your body exhausted."

"I think you exhausting my body is the real way this whole thing began."

"Technically, it began with you asking if I wanted to do great things to your ass."

"Oh, that's selective memory at its finest right there." He lifts me off the ground and I wrap my legs around his waist. "Take me upstairs."

The tub is big enough for me to stretch my legs all the way out and lean against his chest. I rest my forearms on his bent knees, protruding from the water. His hands cup my breasts and tease my nipples. "You ever consider getting these pierced?"

"I just agreed to clamps. Can't you be happy with one victory before you start plotting the next battle?"

"I'm just saying they would look incredibly cute."

"Oh, yeah, then for the rest of my life, I could ask guys if they wanted to see my incredibly cute tits."

"The answer would be yes, but I'd rather not think about you and any future guys right now."

"Hey, I might have a harem someday. Maybe you'll still be around."

"If I'm lucky."

"Your words, not mine."

He pinches and I close my eyes, try not to tense against him. "Let go, beautiful. You know I've got you."

I do. And he does. He has me melting into him from the endorphin rush, but his hand doesn't slide between my legs afterward. "Let's get out and dry off," he says. "I want to play a game."

"What kind of game?"

"Hide and seek."

"Who hides?"

"You hide."

"What if you don't find me?"

"I will. Pick a place where you don't mind being fucked because that's what's happening when I do."

"You have an unfair advantage. I don't know all the house's hiding spots."

"We're not playing in the house."

I sincerely wish that didn't turn me on as much as it does. We put on easy clothes—sleep shorts and a tank for me, and pajama pants and a tank for him. No underwear for anybody. "I'm only going to count to fifty, so think quick. You'll hear the door open, and then my footsteps on the outside stairs, coming to find you."

"If you find me."

"One. Two."

"You can't start yet."

"Three."

Shit. I run down to the living room and out the door. The main bedroom is on the back side of the house, facing the water, so I know he can't see me through a window when I take the outside stairs. I pause at the bottom. If I go behind the house, he might see me through a window. He's moving around inside as he counts. I can hear a soft thud as he steps on every interior stair coming down. My heart races.

He has close neighbors so I can't hide on the side of the house, but I can't go too far, definitely not all the way down to the wooden walkway that leads to the beach. Those rattlesnake warning signs are there for a reason. And I can't go all the way to the sand because sand flies are real, and all tiny biting things are drawn to me. The house is on stilts but there's nowhere to hide under here. It's where we parked. I could hide in his Jeep if I'd thought to grab his keys. Safest place for sex, too. *Dammit.* Why'd I panic and rush out so fast?

The front door opens. There's no way he counted to fifty. The deck creaks as he walks across it. He's going to be on the stairs in a matter of seconds. I spot a plastic five-gallon bucket, grab it, and run to the outdoor shower at the side of the drive-way. It's walled-in with wooden fencing but the vertical planks don't go all the way to the ground. He'd be able to see my ankles and my feet, but not if I stand on this bucket. As gently as I can, I set the bucket upside down on the ground. He's got to be halfway down the stairs already. I slide the latch into place as quietly as possible, hop up onto the bucket, and stretch my arms out to brace myself with each hand against the opposite wall.

His feet hit the ground at the bottom of the stairs. I'm positive because he does it with a jump to be sure I can hear both feet come down on the concrete. "Here, kitty, kitty, kitty."

He's trying to get me to react. No way am I going to make it that easy for him.

"I'm coming to find you."

He's going the wrong way.

"Come out, sweet, little kitty. Let's play." His voice is fading.

Yes! I don't move. We didn't stipulate where base was, but I assume I'm safe if I make it back inside. How long should I wait, though? I'm going to hold out a little longer. I'll be inside sipping wine and watching TV by the time he gets back upstairs. I just need to make sure he's gone far enough. I try to peek through the slats but they're positioned too tightly together. It's not like someone is going to take a naked shower in here. It's just for washing off sand and saltwater.

There's got to be a tiny sliver of space somewhere. There are lights on the exterior of the house. If he's moving around out there, I'd be able to see him, his shadow, at least. I hunch down and try to see through a lower section of the boards. Was that him? Something moved by a bush. It's a cat. I should've known. Why would Wick be crawling? He's not the one who's hiding.

A June bug hits the wall next to my head and I flinch. Why are they even still around? It's not even June anymore. And why did it divebomb me like that? It's like a tiny flying spy, trying to force me to give myself away. Nice try, you little winged snitch. It flies off and I lean forward, listening for footsteps. I swear I think I can hear him breathing.

Holding my own breath, I move my ear closer to the wall. He reaches up and grabs my ankle from behind and I scream!

I jerk my foot away, but the bucket wobbles beneath me and I lose my balance so I have to jump down. He's laughing and I'm trying to recover from the heart attack he just gave me.

He stands on the opposite side of the wall, and I watch his feet walk slowly around toward the door to the shower. There's a pronounced beat between each knock to make it seem ominous.

Knock.

Knock.

Knock.

Uh-uh, no way. I cower against the back wall. He hasn't got me yet. I drop to my knees and scramble under and out. I'm barely upright before he's on me, pinning my arms above my head. "Were you trying to cheat, kitten? Trying to outrun me and take my prize?"

"How can you move that fast?"

"I'm agile, like a cat. But you're just a clumsy little kitten."

"If you call me that one more time, I'm going to knee you right in the balls."

He presses his whole body flat against mine. I can't move. "I'm sorry, what was that? I don't think I understood the threat. Show me." I try to get my leg free, but it's pointless. "Say you're sorry for trying to trick me."

"I'm not apologizing for trying to win."

"You had already lost. And now it's time to pay up. We can either do it right here or inside the shower. Your call."

"Inside."

He backs up barely enough for me to pull my back off the wall but he still holds my arms. "I wouldn't try to run again if I were you. You're out of choices. If I have to catch you again, you're mine where you land."

All the fight leaves my body, not because I'm afraid of the way he could overpower me, but because my legs just turned to jelly at the prospect. I step through the door of the shower and he follows me in. "Close the door," I say.

"No one is down here but us."

"I'd feel safer if we were enclosed on all sides."

"Who's going to hurt you? I'm not going to hurt you." He steps closer and I instinctively back away. "Where are you going?" he teases, tugging on my waistband. There is nowhere I can go.

"Just close it, make it cozy."

"We'll get cozy when we go back upstairs. Turn around and put your hands on the wall."

Without hesitation, my palms meet the wood. He yanks my hips back and my shorts down.

"How'd you find me so easy?"

"I could smell you . . . your shampoo, your bodywash, your incredibly wet pussy . . . damn, you enjoyed that game, didn't you?"

"How'd you really find me?"

"Next time you try to hide using a camouflage bucket, you should pick a location with something for it to blend into."

"Well, how else was I supposed to keep you from seeing me."

"You could've balanced the edges of your feet and hands on the runners. Used the frame."

"What, and just clung there like a spider monkey?"

"Ooh, are you going to make monkey noises for me?"

"Not under any circumstances."

He rubs his warm hand over my ass. "I would've always looked in the shower, beautiful. It's the safest spot."

What does he mean by that? I'm not someone who goes for the safest option. I take risks. I'm a badass, fearless woman. Until I hear the sound of a cap snapping open behind me. I look back to see if it's what I think it is. "You actually did bring lube?"

"I actually did."

"How did I not feel that when you were pressed against me?"

"Back pocket."

"Men get all the pockets! Why do pajamas need back pockets?"

"For surprise lube, obviously."

I laugh. "Yeah, I'm sure that's exactly what it says on the pattern at the factory. Surprise lube pocket."

"Winner's choice pocket." He squeezes the cold gel onto two fingers and presses them right against my backdoor, working them in slowly to the second knuckle. "Is this okay?"

"Last night you said we should take our time and work up to this."

"It's been a whole day. You didn't answer my question."

"Yeah, it's okay. So far."

His fingers withdraw until the tips are all that's touching me, and he squeezes more lube over them before sliding them back in, starting to spiral in and out, reaming me. I drop my head and breathe through the pressure. He adds another round of lube and his fingers slide all the way in easily. After a few more minutes, he pulls them out completely and positions the tip of his cock at my opening. He pushes in just enough to engage our bodies. "You still good?"

"Yeah."

"It's up to you how deep it goes. You have to back up to show me how much is okay."

I press my hips back a little and take what feels like another inch or so. The stretch is intense so I pause to adjust to it. It's been a while since I've done this. He squeezes lube onto his cock and it runs down his hot skin to pool where I'm holding him in place. The added slickness isn't going to help much if I don't slide back to take it in. Wick groans when I do, but he doesn't thrust; he let's me stay in control. He's doing it the right way. My body's relaxing, trust playing a major role in reducing the physical and mental anxiety. I back up again, going farther this time, but he's not all the way in. "I think that's all I can take."

He grips my hips, his thumbs rubbing circles over my skin. "Can I move?" he asks, and I can hear the restraint in his voice.

"Yes. But only to here, okay?"

"I know how far. I promise."

His movements are slow and measured, but like before, my body adjusts to the fullness and he reads the relaxation. Even then, he doesn't try to push beyond the limit I set, but he does increase his pace. "You like the way my cock feels in your ass?"

"Yes, Daddy." It feels so much more risqué to say that out here. There is no one outside the neighboring houses, and even if there were, I didn't say it loud enough for anyone other than us to hear, but it still adds a level of brazenness. And we both like it. Our kinks line up, there is no doubt—even the ones I wasn't aware of before him.

"This tight little ass is mine inside the gym and out, isn't it?"

"All yours. Just in different ways."

"Oh, yeah? You don't think I'd fuck your ass in the gym?"

"You're way too uptight and serious there. All business, all the time." Such an exaggeration, but it provokes him in exactly the way I intended.

"I keep telling you, you've got to be careful how you wield that gauntlet. But I mean business right now, beautiful." He increases his pace slightly again. We're still good, but I'm not sure I want much more speed than this.

His movements become jerky, and he groans again, but it comes out with a stutter this time, ensuring I don't have to worry about him increasing anything.

He didn't hurt me, but I'm relieved at the decreasing pressure. That was enough for a reintroduction to anal. "Stay like this. I left a towel on the stairs."

"You brought a towel out with you?"

"Did you forget what a gentleman I am?"

"Forgive me for underestimating you."

When he returns with the towel, he bites my neck from behind and says, "Never underestimate me."

"Likewise."

"Oh, I wouldn't dream of underestimating you, beautiful."

TWENTY-THREE
DOUBLE STUFF

I t seems like we've been at the beach for longer than a weekend. We know each other a lot better than when we got here. Going out of town with someone when a relationship is new always accelerates it. Or completely wrecks it.

I reach for my bag when we're leaving the house but Wick steps in front me and picks it up. "I've got it." I let him carry it, understanding that he's not doing it because he thinks I'm incapable of carrying it; he just has generations of southern boy expectations woven into his DNA.

After we undid all his storm prep, we ate one last meal on the island, and when I listen to Marlise's voicemail after he drops me off at my place, I'm glad we did because I won't be able to eat anything else today. I have to listen to it twice before I can call her back.

"Why does he want to talk to Heath?"

"Apparently, Mr. Blackwell got tangled up with a difficult partner in the past, which I think you can relate to, and he wants to feel Heath out for himself, make sure he really wants out and you're not forcing his hand. He's also had people back out at the last minute and doesn't want his time wasted. I think he just wants to be sure all parties are serious and willing."

"Heath is a loose cannon. There is no telling what he'll say."

"That could end up working in your favor. It won't take him long to figure out Heath doesn't have any business sense."

"Which will make me look like I don't have any either since I'm the one who went into business with him."

"Well, there's nothing we can do to mitigate that."

"Thanks."

"You're not paying me to blow smoke up your ass."

"It's a good thing." She tells me not to worry until there's a reason. I'm pretty sure this impending conversation between Greg Blackwell and my dipshit ex is a reason. "So, he's going to call Heath and I just have to sit on pins and needles until it happens."

"Email. So there's that to be thankful for."

"Unless they set up a face-to-face via email."

"I don't get the impression Mr. Blackwell takes a lot of face-to-face meetings with strangers. You must've made a good first impression."

"I'd like to think I always do that."

"I didn't call to upset you, but I didn't want to keep it from you either."

"No, I know. Thanks. Any idea when the email will be sent?"

"He didn't give any indication but I'd assume right away, not that people always act according to my assumptions. At any rate, I gave him the requested information. Ball's in his court now."

"It's been in his court."

"And he'll lob it back when he's ready."

Sometimes, Marlise is a woman of few words, but she never fails to make every word count. I know she's right. Greg will respond on his own schedule. It could be as soon as tomorrow, but if I were a betting woman, I'd say this is going to be a very long, nerve-wracking week. Speaking of bets . . .

Me: *Are we even now?*

Wick: *???*

Me: *Winner gets to choose? Ringing any bells yet?*

Wick: *You're all paid up on bet number two after hide-and-seek.*

I did enjoy that game. At least I have the memories from the beach to get me through this week.

Me: *And you're finally done being nice to me?*

Wick: *That was bet number one. In addition to, not instead of. Ringing any bells yet?*

It's ringing something, that's for sure.

Me: *So arrogant.*

Wick: *I like you too.*

I laugh and set my phone aside. Groceries would be a good idea. I'm facing down a week that calls for snacks. Plus, the grocery store is neutral ground for life's bullshit. The worst thing that ever happens there is when they give you your total at the register.

Okay, so I was wrong. The worst thing that happens at the grocery store is trying to find a damn parking space. This is why I usually shop in the middle of the week, or have them delivered. The back-up lights on a car three spaces from the front blink on, and that spot is mine. *Rockstar parking. Damn. I'm getting the name-brand snacks today.*

I'm debating whether Oreo Thins are a healthier choice than regular Oreos, knowing I'd probably just eat twice as many, when someone bumps my cart. Hard.

Oh, hell no. What is he doing in my grocery store?

"Saw your picture on the beach. So, how long has that been going on?"

"How'd you know I was in here?"

He holds up his phone. "It was your idea to share our locations."

How could I have forgotten to block him from that? Of all things. "Yeah, when we were dating. Why would you check it now? Were you stalking me all weekend?"

"No, I just checked twenty minutes ago for the first time in weeks."

"Heath, I didn't even post any pics from the beach. You're obviously lying and you're just fishing to see who I was there with."

"I know who you were there with, Nadine. He's the one who posted your picture." He shows it to me.

Yep, that's me. Sitting on the beach, looking like I don't have a care in the world. And my biggest problem is standing right here, waving it in my face. I never even knew Wick took my picture.

"Can you hold your phone still, please?" I want to read the caption. Maybe he doesn't have to know we were there together-together. Can I spin this somehow? Nope. Not when the caption says: *Nothing beats time spent in a beautiful place with a beautiful woman.* There are whitecaps in the background. I can hear them crashing and rolling in to shore.

"Glad it makes you so happy."

Shit. I didn't mean to smile at it, but yeah, good memories. "It's none of your business who I spend time with."

"I just want to know how long you were fucking him behind my back."

"Will you keep your voice down, please? There are kids in here."

"How long?"

"I told you I was going to use your prepaid training sessions. That's when we started hanging out, okay? There was nothing happening between us while you and I were dating. But we're no longer dating, so who I spend my time with doesn't concern you."

"Why him? So many guys in this city, but you just had to go for him?"

"Okay, for your information, he went for me!"

"I should've known better than to ever trust you."

"Trust? You sure that's a topic you want to discuss with me?"

"Are you fucking the guy who sent me the email, too?"

"You got the email already? Did you reply?"

"Not yet."

"Could you please be professional when you do? This is in your best interest. You know that."

"When you said you were going to secure funding, you failed to mention you were replacing me with a new partner."

"His buyout will be the funding."

"Our buy and sell agreement states that you're supposed to buy me out."

"If you had read it all, you'd know there's a provision for bringing in an outside buyer. Marlise ran it by corporate and they gave it the green light. Greg Blackwell already owns a franchise. This could be seamless, Heath."

"Seems like Marlise only has your interests in mind. Maybe I need to get my own attorney."

"Marlise isn't going to screw you. She can't. I already told you she'll show you the numbers." The picture is still open on his phone. He's going to be a child about this every step of the way. "If you want to have another attorney look over everything, go for it, but could you hire one quickly before Greg decides it would be easier to just open a new store on his own?"

"Oh, you're on a first-name basis with him. Nice."

"Again, no one is conspiring against you. This is a chance for you to cash out, put all your money in Bounty of the Seas."

"I need to think about some things." He looks at his phone

again. "Maybe we should've put something in our agreement about you not being a whore."

Do not throw the Oreos. Do not throw the Oreos. Do not throw the Oreos.

Why would it not have occurred to Wick to ask me before he posted that picture? Before he even took it? Arrogance. I put the Oreo Thins in my cart. Two packages. I better not regret this.

TWENTY-FOUR
STAYIN' ALIVE

On Monday morning, I resume my training sessions with Wick. He catches me on my way out and says, "Hey, my next session just canceled. Do you have time to go to breakfast?"

This is perfect because I've withheld my complaints about the photo he posted because this didn't feel like the time or place, but I have to get it off my chest. "Yeah. I need to talk to you about something anyway."

"If you're about to tell me you don't want to see me anymore, I'm really going to regret not working you harder this morning."

"It's not that, I promise." I know he's going to freak out about Heath tracking me to the store, but we need to have this conversation.

We meet at a nearby café and I keep things light until after our coffees hit the table and we've each had our first sips. "So, somebody saw a picture you posted of me. From the beach."

"Name this elusive somebody."

"Heath."

"He'll get over it. I guess he's still following me because I didn't even tag you."

"Yeah, about that. I'm not cool with having my picture taken and posted without my consent."

His jaw tightens. "It's not a nude. I like candid photos. I'd much rather capture you enjoying yourself than posing for the camera."

"I can appreciate that part. But you can't post them without my permission. Especially now with everything that's going on with Heath. He's convinced you and I were seeing each other while I was still with him."

"Fuck him. It's none of his business when we started seeing each other. If he calls to whine about it again, just don't take his call. Block his number."

"I can't block him, Wick. We're still partners and I need to do everything in my power not to upset him until we're not. Besides, he didn't call me. I saw him." I can read the conclusions he's jumping to all over his face. "I'd neglected to block him from tracking my location. He blindsided me in the grocery store. I was caught off-guard and almost let it get out of hand."

"He stalked you?"

"Listen to me, please. Greg has reached out to him but Heath hasn't responded. Whatever he says when he does could influence whether or not Greg buys him out. If I don't walk a fine line right now to keep Heath on an even keel, it could cause me to lose the store entirely."

Our plates come out and Wick douses his omelet in hot sauce. "I promise I will not post any more pictures of you without your permission." He shoves a giant bite into his mouth, chews like he'd rather punch something.

"I need you to also promise you won't interact with Heath."

He takes a gulp of his coffee, and then pulls his phone out of his pocket. "Blocking him everywhere right now. Done. I couldn't interact with him now if I wanted to."

"Thank you. I read your caption on the picture. That was a really nice thing to say."

"It was the truth. Eat those eggs. You can't live on carbs alone."

"I eat protein all the time."

He raises his eyebrows. "How many arguments do we have to have this morning?"

"Were we arguing? Because I didn't hear any argument."

"Because I kept it on the inside. Because I care about you. But as soon as this buy out is finalized, all bets are off."

"What happens then? We're going to have the mother of all arguments?"

"Then, I'll make my own decisions about how and when I interact with him."

"Does this macho jock shit have an expiration date?"

"No. Are you sure you don't want to meet Liam, come hang out with us for a while tonight?"

"He's only here for a few days, and he didn't come to town to meet me. Go relive your glory days and retell all your tales of debauchery." I take a bite of my eggs. "But y'all are welcome to join me, Oakley and Garth downtown for disco night tomorrow."

"Is Hollis going?" He finishes off his omelet while I take my second bite of scrambled eggs.

"No. It's not really his thing."

"Thank God, because it's definitely not mine. I just needed to know if I was going to look like a bad boyfriend in comparison." *Oh, that beach trip jumped you right to boyfriend, huh?* I don't mention it. It's not like I'm seeing anyone else, or want to. Not sure I'm ready for the label of girlfriend yet, but I've never been big on labels.

We kiss goodbye in the parking lot and I make one last thing clear. "If you ever sneak naked photos of me, I will sedate you and remove your testicles with nail clippers."

"Thanks for offering to sedate me first, I guess?"

"If you weren't so strong, sedation would be off the table."

"I would never take nude pictures of you without your clear consent. Not ever."

I cross items off my mental checklist as I drive away from the café. We've had the secret-picture-taking conversation. Heath's ability to track my location has officially been disabled. Wick has promised to stay away from him. The only thing I have left to worry about regarding Heath is his response to Greg. And whether or not he'll really hire an attorney and drag this out. Marlise thinks he was just blowing off steam. I guess time will tell.

There are no new developments by Tuesday evening when I'm getting ready to go out with Oakley and Garth. They'll have a fit if I don't totally cosplay Studio 54 circa 1978 with them, so I'm wearing a vintage, knee-length red halter dress with a plunging neckline. Kudos to my aunt who saved every dress she owned from the seventies, and to the inventor of boob tape, because that will be the only thing saving me from a nip-slip tonight. I reconsider the shoes my aunt insisted had to be worn with this dress. The straps pinch a little, but they do look good.

When they pick me up, Oakley is gorgeous in gold lamé, and Garth looks like he should be on the billboard advertising this event. He's the only one of us who has a collar, and it's so big it deserves its own zip code.

These strappy heels may look good with this dress but they were not made for dancing all night. "How did women in the seventies wear these things?" I unbuckle them in the car on the way home.

"Their feet were probably numb from all the cocaine," Oakley says.

Garth looks across the backseat. "Girl! You're going to get my Uber account suspended. Again." He looks to the driver, apologizes, and assures him we did not bring any drugs into his car.

I scoff at his paranoia. We got ketchup on the backseat of one nitpicky driver, and now Garth thinks we're a rideshare risk. This driver laughs and asks us about disco night. Then he proceeds to share his own drug-addled stories from the eighties. By the time he drops me off, I'm grateful to have survived the ride. "Put it in the group text when y'all make it home. Both of you. I mean it."

My bed has never looked so inviting. Me and Monk-Monk snuggle and watch a gruesome unsolved murder case play out on my TV until I know Oakley and Garth are both home safe. I still don't know who the killer is, but I can't hold my eyes open another minute. They've got DNA from the ax handle; they don't need me for this one.

TWENTY-FIVE
PROMISES, PROMISES

W e take advantage of a Wednesday-Addams-themed brunch since I was at the beach Sunday and we're all having slow work weeks. Wake Up with Wednesday is proving to be an excellent mid-week choice. Garth regales us with more stories from last night's driver. He was the last one to be dropped off, and apparently the driver saved his best stories for the end of the ride.

"My feet are still sore," I say, "but this gothic French toast is making me less cranky about it." My plate is a deep shade of purple from the crushed berries and syrup mingling together. The edible flowers are all dark colors and drizzled with darker chocolate.

"I think these blood orange mimosas are what's improving your mood," Oakley says.

"I prefer to think it's the excellent company." Garth pulls a black tater tot off the skewer in his bloody mary and pops it into his mouth. "And on that topic, why didn't you invite Wick and his friend to spooky brunch?"

"We can go a few days without seeing each other." I steal one of his macabre tots. "I'll see him in the morning, bright and early."

Our waitress brings out the mini-cinnamon-roll brains we ordered. It's not like I need more carbs and sugar, but I reach for one, anyway. Oakley pushes the little iron skillet closer to help me out. "Your arms look great, by the way," she says.

"Thanks." I flex to show them off. I catch a man a few tables away smiling at me. It's a nice smile but there's no cocky challenge quirking at the corners. I'm immune to him. Would I have always been? He's kind of hot, kind of my type: longish dark hair, full-sleeve tats, face full of scruff . . . yeah, it's doing nothing for me. If someone had shown me a picture of that guy a few years ago, I'd have asked if I could keep it. Okay, a few months ago. I've been transformed by a man with a fresh and clean look—and dirtier actions than anyone *my type* ever exhibited. Who knew?

My phone lights up on the table. "Oh, shit. It's Marlise. This could be it, y'all. I'm scared to answer it. What if Heath blew everything?"

Oakley bounces in her seat. "What if he didn't? Pick it up!"

"I will answer that phone for you if you don't grab it right now." Garth's hand encroaches.

I bring the phone to my ear. "Hello."

"Were you out with your new boyfriend last night?"

"No. I danced the night away with Oakley and Garth."

"Have you talked to him this morning?"

"Why are you asking me about Wick?"

"Apparently, he and Heath got into an altercation."

"No. No, no, no, no, no. He promised me that wouldn't happen."

"Well, we all know what promises were made for. All I can tell you is I just got off the phone with Heath and he says he was humiliated and threatened in public, and we are to funnel all further communication through his attorney. Which he definitely now has. I have the guy's contact information."

Champagne and cinnamon churn in my stomach. "How could he have done this?"

"You need to talk to him. Get his version of how it happened. I told you before, I don't like surprises."

"It's not like I could've predicted this. And I wasn't there to prevent it. One of Wick's old teammates is in town and—"

"Ah, there we go. He went out drinking with an old buddy and their testosterone levels rose right along with their blood alcohol levels, and either they found Heath or he found them, and I think we can puzzle out the rest. But get his goddamn side of the story, anyway. If there was anything beyond threats and humiliation, we need to know. I'm talking so much as a slap or a shove. Ask the question directly."

"I'm so sorry, Marlise."

"Apologizing for a man is a bad habit to fall into. Don't start. See what he has to say and get back to me."

Garth and Oakley sit frozen in their seats. What are they supposed to say? I don't even know what to say about it. "I guess y'all could hear all that?"

Oakley nods. "Marlise doesn't exactly have a soft voice."

"Right." I throw my napkin onto my plate. There's no point in taking my food to go. My stomach is in knots. "I've got to go home. I can't call Wick from here."

"I'll get the Uber." Garth already has his phone out. We don't always get a ride to brunch but the parking sucks here, so it's a fortunate accident I don't have to drive myself home. There's no way I could manage it right now. I'm not sure I could stand if Oakley didn't have her hand on my arm, guiding me through it. My head is spinning. How could Wick have done this?

When the car pulls to the curb in front of my house, Oakley announces she's coming in. I don't argue.

I sit on my couch and attempt to collect myself for a few minutes. Oakley grabs Monk-Monk from my bedroom and drops him in my lap. My emotional support monkey. "Put it on speaker," she says. "I'll stay out of it, I promise."

It's not like I can hold onto the phone, anyway, not with the way my hands are still shaking. I turn the volume all the way up and set it on the coffee table.

"Hey, beautiful. Can I call you back in a few? I just got in line to drop Liam at the airport."

"No, you cannot call me back. But you might want to tell your friend to go ahead and get out of the car because this about to get ugly. Tell me exactly what happened between you and Heath last night."

"He fucking called you to whine about that shit? That little punk ass—"

"He got an attorney, Wick."

"I've got an attorney, too. Tell him I said bring it!"

"He's not bringing it to you, you idiot! He's taking it out on me. Marlise is the one who had to tell me. We're only speaking through our attorneys now. There is no way he'll be cooperative after what you did. I'm going to lose the store because of you!"

"Bullshit. He just wants attention, same as he did last night. Liam and I were minding our own business, having a good time, and the next thing I know, Heath appears out of nowhere and gets all up in my face talking shit about how I betrayed him but I can have you now because he doesn't even want you anymore. He's lucky he didn't leave that bar in an ambulance." I hear Liam tell Heath to pull over. "Are you at home?"

"Yeah, I'm at home, trying to figure out how the hell I'm going to fix everything you screwed up."

"Just sit tight. I'll head your way as soon as I leave the airport."

"You are the last person I want to see right now. I just need to know if you hit him. Or put your hands on him at all, even to shove him away. Did you have any physical contact?"

"No, but I wanted to. And now I want to all over again."

"Stay. Away. From him."

"I didn't go near him last night. He came running up on me."

"And you just couldn't let it go."

"Apparently not."

"We're done. I never want to see you again."

"Don't be dramatic, Nadine. You're pissed. I get it, but—"

I end the call, and throw Monk-Monk across the room, knocking my trio of hear-no-evil, see-no-evil, speak-no-evil, pin-up-girl figures off a shelf.

Oakley walks over, picks them all up, and sets them right again. If only righting everything were that easy. She hugs Monk-Monk on her way back to the couch. "Do you want my opinion or for me to just sit here and keep my mouth shut?"

She only asks that question when she knows I'm not going to like her opinion.

"How can you take his side in this?"

"I'm not taking his side, but I think you should sit down with him and let him tell you the whole story. And then you can explain to him the seriousness of what this might've caused. I don't think either of you understands the other's reaction right now. Talk it out."

"He promised me."

"Honestly, Nade, I would've gone off on Heath, too. He was never Prince Charming, but he's become a completely obnoxious, entitled prick, who thinks he can do whatever he wants. He needed to be brought down a peg or two."

"And if my business gets brought down in the process, who cares, right?"

"You know I care about that. I care about everything that matters to you. And I think Wick matters to you a whole lot more than you want to admit. That's why this hurts so much. It's not just about your business."

"He lied. He said he wouldn't confront him and then he turned right around and did it."

"It sounds more like he got confronted and he reacted in the heat of the moment."

"Reacted like a complete fucking Neanderthal."

"Without seeing video footage of the incident, I'm going to have to call that an assumption."

"You're not being interviewed for a jury here, Oakley. You could be a little less impartial."

"He may have lost control, said some things that made a bad situation worse, but Heath is the reason the bad situation existed to begin with. I really think Wick's a good guy."

"Doesn't make him good for me, though, does it? I'm sure I'll get by without him. I walked away from a good man before and it didn't kill me."

My phone buzzes. I reject the call. He calls right back. I deny him again. He texts. I delete it. "How am I supposed to call Marlise back if he won't stop blowing up my damn phone?"

Oakley calls Marlise on her phone, and hands it to me.

I relay Wick's side of the story, and tell her he says the altercation didn't get physical in any way. "Do you know if Heath responded to Greg's email before all this? Or after? At any point?"

"We didn't cover that. He was too busy telling me how he's going to sue your boyfriend for libel. I was too professional to tell him the term he was looking for is slander, not libel. Or that he doesn't have a case for either one. As long as nobody put hands on anybody, this is a non-issue."

"It doesn't matter if he can win a frivolous lawsuit or not. He could scare Greg off with his dumbass behavior."

"Heath is a noisemaker. Greg is an intelligent business-man. I'll make a call in the morning."

"What are you going to say to him?"

"I'm going to remind him that your store is making money

and point out the fact that only happens when businesses are being run well. And then I'll bluntly state that Heath is dead-weight and you're looking to cut him, like anyone with any business sense would, but he's quickly becoming a liability and you need to move forward, one way or another."

"Are you sure trying to force his hand is the right move?" My phone lights up again and I turn it off.

"Not sure his hand can be forced, but I think he's a man who appreciates being informed. And I don't imagine he likes to be ignored, so I will pointedly ask if Heath has both-ered to reply to his email yet. I'll let him know Heath is behaving erratically of late, interfering in your personal life, and acting like a clown in public. We get ahead of the fool-ishness and show Greg you've got a firm hold on what matters. I still think Heath will jump all over the deal if Greg pulls the trigger. He's got more reason to be money-moti-vated than anything else. He's just flexing his muscles on his way out."

Oakley nods along like she's part of my legal team. I know Marlise is making sense, but finding out about Wick and me wounded Heath's pride. I guess I just have to hope he wants the money more than he wants to prove a point. "What is it with men and their pissing contests?"

"Hell if I know, but I reckon Heath is about piss-broke at this point, so I don't know how much longer he can afford to hold on. Having said that, I've seen dumber than him make a miraculous comeback when he got counted out too soon. You stay on your game."

"What choice do I have?"

"Not much." I wince at her candor. "I hope you weren't too hard on your new man. I'm sure Heath had it coming. The timing just wasn't great."

Oakley's nodding becomes more vigorous. I look away from her.

"I don't think the new man was so great overall. I've got

too much going on to be trying to start a new relationship right now, anyway."

"Huh. I always found a readily available dick to be useful during trying times. But you know yourself better than I do, and I guess you probably don't have any trouble finding a man when you want one."

"What the fuck is that supposed to mean!"

"That you're young and attractive? Have a glass of wine, honey. This too shall pass."

I give Oakley her phone back. "Does dick come up that often in conversation when you talk to her?"

"To be fair, she sort of treats Hollis like a son, so I doubt she really wants to talk about dick with me."

"True. I guess his is less generic."

"Definitely name-brand dick. I didn't put that shit on lock for nothing."

Only Oakley could make me laugh right now. When I finally convince her I'm okay and it's fine to call Hollis to come pick her up, I turn my phone back on. It takes less than two seconds for Wick's next attempt to come through. I turn it right back off.

Before she walks out, Oakley says, "You can't leave your phone off. What if there's an emergency?"

"I love you. Go home."

TWENTY-SIX
HE HAD IT COMING

Several hours pass before I cautiously turn my phone back on. No incoming call or text vibrates my hand. Wick hasn't show up at my door. At least he can respect one boundary.

Hurricane Nadine has made landfall on South Padre. I watch a few videos of the raging winds, complete with a lunatic reporter clinging to a stop sign to keep from being blown away. There is not enough money in the world for me to put myself in harm's way like that, or to look like that much of a fool in front of a camera. It's almost always a man. *Oooh, look how brave I am!* Stupid dumbass idiot showboating fuckwits. All of them. I'm done.

Wick: *Will I see you at the gym in the morning?*

delete

I should block him and get it over with.

Oakley: *Come over for dinner?*

Me: *Just ordered food. But thanks.*

The last thing I want is food, but I don't want anyone worrying about me either. I'm fine.

Before I go to bed, I watch a few more hurricane videos. The storm surge is coming on now. No more reporters or camera crews in the street, just footage captured by security cameras. My God, it's devastating. The recovery is going to take months, maybe longer. When the sun comes up tomorrow, nothing is going to look the same.

Dealing with people the past few days has been a joy. All the jokes comparing me to the hurricane that's left South Padre destroyed are pure comedy gold, and so uplifting. Yay, let's laugh about a natural disaster whose true cost isn't even known yet. In my head, I've watched them all be sucked up by tornadoes and carried away. But outwardly, my smile hasn't faltered.

Maybe I should take some vacation time and go help the recovery efforts. It's too soon yet, but when they start letting people come in to rebuild, I could do that. My email to corporate about coordinating donations from other franchisees hasn't been answered yet. I'll donate from my store, anyway.

It's still mine. And Heath's. I should probably have Marlise reach out to his attorney to get his okay before sending cases of juice down there. I'm not supposed to make any big decisions without him, and to Heath, every little thing has become a big decision. He won't object to it; he'll probably announce it on his website. My bigger concern should be making sure he doesn't try to send any BOTS products as part of our donation. He definitely cannot go down there to make the delivery. I can see him now, giving his pitch to storm victims, trying to add them to his downline.

Greg Blackwell is probably already planning to donate, but I've sworn not to reach out to him on my own again. Marlise has been in contact with him. He still hasn't made a decision. I know Heath and I knee-jerked and jumped into our franchise without enough consideration, but Greg is all about taking his time. As a kid, he probably counted his macaroni before he ate it, and rejected the pieces that weren't curled to the right degree.

If he decides to become my partner, I'm sure I'll appreciate his discerning approach, but right now, I just need him to take a leap of faith, trust his gut. His initial instinct was to like me, I know it was. He's not the type of person who would linger over conversation with someone if his first impression was negative, not a man who's big on giving second-chances. We have that in common. We're like-minded; we'd be great business partners.

Wick: *Will you meet me somewhere for a drink? Just hear me out?*

He hasn't tried to contact me all day, but I should've known he wouldn't let the week end peacefully. It's my own fault.

Me: *Never want to see you again. Ringing any bells?*
block number

My weekend is booked. Tonight, I'm solving murders, might kill a bottle of wine while I'm at it; tomorrow, I have to go to the carwash and the grocery store, clean, do laundry, and there are emails and paperwork that need my attention; Sunday, we're back to our regularly scheduled brunch routine, and then I'm hanging out with Oakley in her pool all afternoon. So busy.

I change into pajamas and order a pizza and a salad. Balance. I'm all about it.

Yelling at the TV might not keep the girl from getting in the car with the psycho, or make the detective see the evidence right in front of his face, but it's a form of therapy. Not instead of, in addition to.

"He's lying! Get a warrant for his phone!" This guy's going to prison. I love when they're so smug, thinking just because they deleted the texts, they're gone. He's about to get his ass kicked by digital forensics. "Okay, yes! Good job, guys. Keep smiling, motherfucker. They've got you dead to rights and you don't even know it. That ego is about to be your ultimate downfall."

God, I love a good camera angle on a perp walk. "You look better in handcuffs, baby!"

The prosecution better not have whiffed on this one. "No deal. First degree or nothing. I will riot right here on this couch!"

"Yes! Say goodbye to your yacht, pretty boy! For-ev-errrr!"

Damn, that was satisfying. I debate whether I should tempt fate and watch another episode or go to bed on a high note. I've got a full day tomorrow. I should probably turn in.

Well, damn, I took too long; the next one's already started. I'll go to bed after the verdict on this one. Or the one after.

TWENTY-SEVEN
BLOOD IN THE WATER

W hen the mop starts to come apart, it's time to stop mopping. I might have been a little vigorous. There is nothing left to clean, no emails that need a response, no laundry to do . . . there isn't anything left to check off my to-do list. I either need to go to the gym, sit down and relax, or dye my hair. Bangs?

Wick might be at the gym, so that's not happening. Every time I try to relax, I think about his arrogant ass telling me I don't know how and then I want to claw his fucking eyes out. *Feisty kitten. Get out of my head, asshole!*

I don't have any hair dye. I do, however, have scissors . . . who the hell is knocking on my door? Probably the universe saving me from bangs. Momentarily, anyway.

The guy at my front door is entirely too young to look so beaten down by life. There is a box truck idling at the curb. "Hey, I just need to make sure the gate isn't locked and there are no animals in the backyard before we head back there to set up."

"You're at the wrong address."

He looks at the numbers above my door, and says, "No, this is the right house."

"I can guarantee you it's not. Whatever it is you're supposed to set up belongs somewhere else."

He looks at the tablet in his hand. "Are you Nadine Garrison?"

"Yes, but—"

"Listen, I don't know why anybody rents an inflatable hot tub when it's a thousand degrees outside, but you're getting one because that's what the order says." He hands me a damp business card from his sweat-soaked shirt pocket. "You don't want it in your yard? Call that number and they can send another crew out to take it away. But it's our job to deliver it."

He sent me a hot tub? Some guys would've tried their luck with roses. He's insane. Certifiable. "Fine. No lock on the gate. No pets. Knock yourselves out."

The thing inflates pretty quickly but it takes a while to fill from the hose. My water bill is going to be outrageous. Most inconsiderate gift ever. The delivery guys toss some chlorine tabs in as it fills. When the water rises above the jets, the young one turns it on and shows me how the controls work. "It'll take several hours to heat up." He sticks his hand in like he's testing the temperature but he doesn't seem to want to take it out. I think he's just trying to cool off a little.

"Do y'all want some cold water?"

"Please."

They both go through a couple glasses of water before they turn off the hose and tell me to enjoy it. "When are you coming back for it?"

"No idea. You'd have to ask the office, or ask whoever ordered it for you."

"How long do people usually rent them for?"

"Usually, a day or a weekend, but it can be longer." He asks me to sign on the screen to confirm delivery.

The two men slide the cover into place and walk back through the gate. I listen to their truck rumble off down the street, and blink a few times to be sure I didn't just imagine this whole encounter, but there is definitely a hot tub in my yard.

I leave to run errands with no specific stops in mind. Might buy a new bathing suit to christen my temporary hot tub, might buy some hair dye. The day is young. What I won't be doing is acknowledging anything for Wick. I'm sure the company will let him know they've delivered it.

As I drive, my shock turns to anger. What an arrogant gesture. Who just assumes they can have something delivered that will take up that much space in someone's back yard? Not to mention assuming I'd be home to receive it. I could've been away on a trip. What if my lease had a No Portable Hot Tubs clause? So arrogant.

I skip the hair dye and book an appointment at the salon for next week instead. The last time I dyed my hair myself, I cried for two hours after I saw the results, and then I spent four hours at the salon getting it corrected. Some mistakes teach hard lessons. It's a shame I can't seem to learn as quickly from my poor judgment in men. Fuck it, I'm getting two bathing suits.

When I get home, I dig out the rolls of peel-and-stick wallpaper I bought six months ago, and finally create that accent wall I've wanted in my bedroom. Lining up the pattern is exacting and infuriating, but I refuse to give up until it's perfect and my shoulders ache.

Tonight's sunset is extra pink and tangerine with bright violet streaks running through it. I sit outside and contemplate the hot tub. It's not going anywhere tonight and neither am I, so I might as well use it. When I fold back the cover, I'm hoping for warmth, pleasantly surprised to find heat high enough to generate steam.

My bathing suits are all inside but my neighbor's out of town. It's unlikely anyone can see me, anyway. I didn't turn the light on when I came out, and the moon is waning, so it's barely bright enough to see the threadbare clouds separating and drifting apart.

I sink down into the rolling water and try to shut out everything but the stars. I'm apparently more mesmerized by the night sky than I realize because Oakley scares the shit out of me when she barges through my gate. "You're not answering your phone, you don't answer your door—"

"My phone's inside."

She huffs and stomps into my house, presumably to retrieve it for me. No reaction at all to the hot tub. Hollis, who entered the yard right behind her, points at it and says, "Nice."

"It was a gift."

"Even better."

"It'll be gone in a few days. I think."

"A disappearing hot tub. Interesting."

I roll my eyes but I laugh. "Yeah, my life is nothing if not interesting."

Oakley reappears with my phone and sets it on my patio table. She looks at me now like she's seeing the hot tub for the first time. "When did you buy a hot tub?"

"It was gift," Hollis says.

Before I can explain, the gate opens again.

How dare he! How very fucking dare he waltz into my yard with that smile on his face!

"Oh, good, you're using it." He closes the gate behind him, as if he thinks he's staying for a while. He's not. "You would be amazed how hard it is to get a decent bottle of wine delivered in this city on short notice." He holds the bottle out like I might want to read the label. I'm not impressed and I'm not going to be impressed.

"Wish we'd known you were in need," Hollis says. "We got a delivery this afternoon."

"I'm not sure I can afford to shop in your cellar." They

laugh and shake hands like this is some backyard soiree I've invited them all to attend. I didn't invite any of them.

Wick turns his eyes to me, sitting naked in a hot tub I didn't ask for in the midst of an impromptu gathering I didn't plan. "Looks like you haven't opened anything yet. I'll go inside and choose from your plethora of corkscrews to open this one for you."

I'm speechless. Five minutes ago, I think I might've been truly relaxed. This is why I don't let my guard down. The moment you relax, the enemy executes a sneak attack!

Oakley snatches the bottle from his hand. "Better yet, we'll go inside and open it while you get in the hot tub."

Hollis is right on her heels as they disappear into my house. The moment the door shuts behind them, Wick starts shedding his clothes.

"They are right there! What are you doing?"

"I feel pretty confident they've both seen a naked man before. And I would think my intentions would be obvious, but I'm joining you in the hot tub."

"Oh, no you're not!"

He barges right in like a pirate, boarding a ship he's about to plunder. "I'll stay way over here."

"Get out!"

"You get out."

"I'm naked."

"So am I."

"You don't care who sees you naked."

"You won't take my calls, you won't answer my texts—"

"That doesn't give you the right to hold me hostage in a hot tub!"

"You're not being held hostage. But I don't want you to get out. I want you to let me say what I need to say. If you still want me to get out when I'm done, I'll go."

"You are so fucking arr—"

Hollis and Oakley come back out and hand us each a glass

of wine. "I'll leave the bottle here," Hollis says, setting it on the table.

"Now that I know you're safe and not bleeding out in a ditch somewhere, we'll let you get back to your evening," Oakley says.

"Take him back with you."

"He didn't come with us. I'm sure he knows the way out."

Hollis puts his hand on her shoulder. "We genuinely had nothing to do with Wick showing up. But we're leaving."

"They didn't know I was coming over here," Wick says.

"You are all the worst liars in the world!"

Oakley steps to the side of the hot tub and squats down to make eye contact. "Nade, we had no idea, I promise. I panicked because I couldn't reach you. And I think we both know why he's here, so maybe just hear him out."

"Leave."

"On my way." She stands and looks down at Wick. "If I were you, I'd choose my words very carefully."

That's so obviously code for *don't fuck this up*. But he already did that.

The gate latch clicks and we're alone, naked in a hot tub. *Full circle.* He's silent. I certainly don't have anything to say. The clouds are clearing out, making way for more stars to appear.

I try not to look at him but it's killing me that he's just sitting here, saying nothing, and wrecking my peaceful night. When I sneak a glance, of course, he's staring right at me, and I guess eye contact is what he's been waiting for because he starts talking.

"I think if I spent the rest of my life with you, you'd never stop being a challenge."

"This is true. It's who I am, Wick. I'm disagreeable and stubborn and outspoken and—"

"Beautiful. Smart. Strong. Funny. Soft. Sexy. Amazing."

"Let me know when you run out of adjectives. You don't

like to lose. And this was always a game for you. A challenge. You said it right from the start. You're only here now because you can't stand not having the last word."

"Love."

"What?"

"Do I think you might be a challenge to love sometimes? Oh, yeah. I think you might be hard as hell to love sometimes. But I'm going to love you, anyway, whether you're with me or not. So, just be with me."

Pfft, love. Guys always want to pull that word out like it's a get-out-of-jail-free card.

"I can't be with someone who disrespects my boundaries and breaks my trust."

"I didn't go looking for him. But I am a grown man, Nadine. You can have your boundaries but you can't set mine. I promised you I'd leave him alone, which I did until he walked up in my face, talking shit." A piece of his wine glass breaks at the rim where his thumb is smashed against it but he keeps going like he didn't even feel it. "I can say I'm sorry until the world ends, but I need you to understand what I'm apologizing for and what I'm not. I'm not sorry for anything I said to him. I'm still a little sorry I didn't rearrange his fucking face. But I am endlessly sorry that I may have met you at the wrong time. I am sorry that love went wrong and left you scared to try again. I'm sorry the next guy turned out to be a loser. I'm sorry that—"

"You're bleeding." There's a small glass triangle floating in his wine, and a thin rivulet of blood running down his thumb.

"Goddammit! This is why you're not supposed to use glass in a hot tub, Nadine! This is why you need me!"

"For plastic wine glasses?"

"Balance. See, you're just now thinking about buying plastic wine glasses. After somebody got hurt. You're reactive but I'm proactive. I would've already bought the plastic wine glasses."

"Are you saying you think I need someone to protect me from myself?"

"Are we going to talk in circles all night? I'm saying I think we're good together. I'm promising you that I'm a safe choice. I can't make you choose me, but I couldn't walk away without doing this."

"Sending me a hot tub?"

"Talking to you face-to-face, looking into your eyes. If I could promise you that I'll never piss you off this badly again, I would, but I can't because it would be a lie. And I won't lie to you."

My phone rings and I want to ignore it but my gut says it could be Tori, calling from the store. I still have an obligation as the owner until it's officially over. "I have to check that."

He nods like he understands.

I dry my hands on my shirt and reach for my phone. It's not Tori. It's Marlise. My hands are only half dry but they're shaking at full speed. "Hi."

"Hey. Are you out?"

"No, I'm home."

"Are you dressed to go out?"

I look down at my completely undressed body. "Um, not at all."

"Well, you might want to put on a party dress because it looks like you've got yourself a new partner."

"He said yes? Greg actually fucking said yes?"

"He actually fucking said yes."

"And Heath?"

"Champing at the bit."

"Thank you. Thank you, Marlise. For everything." Tears run down my wet face.

"Can you be over here at two o'clock on Wednesday?"

"I'll be there at one-forty-five."

"Celebrate. But don't do anything stupid."

"Who, me?"

"I'll see you Wednesday."

Wick is smiling. "Congratulations."

"Thanks. I need a towel. And you need a towel and a bandage. Come in."

I grab us each a towel and rummage around until I find a box of bandages and a spray-bottle of peroxide.

"It's fine," he says, holding up his thumb. But dots of blood form on his skin as soon as he releases the pressure.

"Fingers bleed forever." I grab his hand and spritz his thumb with peroxide before I wrap the bandage tightly around it.

Wick goes back outside for his clothes, comes back in fully dressed. Because why wait until you're inside to drop your towel and put your clothes on like a normal person? He drapes the towel over the back of a kitchen chair. "I hope your new partnership works out. There aren't words to express how sorry I am that ours didn't. But I'll stop bothering you, let you get on with your life."

He turns to leave and I hear Marlise's voice in my head. *But don't do anything stupid.*

"Hey," I say before he reaches the door.

He stops and slowly faces me again. "Yeah?"

"I want the plastic wine glasses."

"What about the arrogant bastard who comes with them?"

"Oh, I want to kick his ass like you can't even imagine, but I'd rather eat glass than let him walk out of my life right now."

EPILOGUE: ONE YEAR LATER

Wick lets out a long wolf whistle when he finds me in the kitchen of the venue, helping Garth go through Oakley's checklist before the reception dinner begins.

"Don't come in here trying to distract me."

Garth waves me away, "Go, be distracted. I've got this. Members of the wedding party don't need to help."

"I'm not just a member of the wedding party. Besides, I need something to do. I just had to stand still for an hour, smiling for a million pictures."

Wick's arms wrap around my waist. "I never knew what seeing you in a tux would do to me."

"Well, this is not your average tux," I tease, though it's true. Mine is much more fitted and instead of a button-down shirt underneath, I'm wearing a magenta silk camisole.

"I thought the maid of honor wasn't supposed to upstage the bride, but I'm pretty sure all eyes were on you during that ceremony."

"All your eyes. Anyway, I may have upstaged the groom, but Oakley's the most beautiful bride to ever walk down the aisle."

"She does look radiant," Garth agrees. "But you definitely upstaged the groom."

"It's only fair," I say. "I was her original better half. Anyway, he knew we were going to play dueling tuxes."

"You won." Wick kisses my neck.

Garth kicks us out of the kitchen. "Take all that somewhere else before the caterers quit on me."

I give in and let Wick lead me outside. Everything about this venue is perfectly Oakley, from the tree branches dripping with twinkle lights to the horse-drawn carriage she and Hollis will be arriving in soon. Guests are already seated inside, and appetizers and drinks being served to keep them happy.

We sit on a bench near a fountain. "This is nice," I admit. "Guess I did need to sit down and take a breath."

"Yeah, I've hardly seen you the past few weeks."

"Life's been a little crazy." I look up at the lights, twinkling above our heads.

"Let's make it a little crazier."

I laugh that he would think for a minute that tone of voice might work right now. "We are not having sex at . . ." My words evaporate. I can't believe what I'm seeing in his hand. "You're not supposed to get engaged at your best friend's wedding, Wick. Talk about upstaging!"

"How about you say yes first, and then tell me how I did it wrong."

"So arrogant." I shake my head but I couldn't wipe the smile off my face if I tried, and I'm not trying.

"Marry me, Nadine."

"That's supposed to be a question, not a command."

"Coming from a less arrogant man, maybe. But you chose me."

"I did, didn't I? Well, we've come this far, I guess I might as well marry your arrogant ass."

He slips the ring onto my finger and his kiss sweeps me away to that place where only he can take me, where there's nothing but easy silence and the whole world is at bay. Because that's what he does for me.

I stare at the ring, awe-struck at how perfectly right he got it. "It's gorgeous, Wick. But we have to put it back in the box until after Oakley gets home from her honeymoon, okay? We'll announce it then, and I promise I'll make a huge big deal of it, but for now, it has to be just between us."

"We don't have to announce it. But please don't take that ring off."

Fuck. "I feel like I have to."

"She's not going to notice your hand tonight. She's lost in this whole fairytale world she's created." He looks around at the lights and the flowers everywhere. "You said yes."

"Did you really have any doubt I would say yes?"

"Have you met yourself? Even I'm not that arrogant."

"Okay. I'll keep it on, but I'm putting my hand in my pocket every time she comes near."

"Feel free to put it in my pocket, if you want." We kiss until the approaching clip-clop of hooves yanks me back to reality. I hop up and reach for his hand. Come on. It's time to go welcome the bride and groom.

I rest my left hand in my lap as much as possible while we eat, and keep it in my pocket while mingling. The only place I can't inconspicuously hide the ring is on the dance floor. I turn it around so the diamond won't catch the light because I know it would be an instant beacon for Oakley, like her bat signal. And I'm sure she would respond in record time.

We find Greg in the crowd. As soon as he sees me, he says, "Howdy, partner." *Yeah, that never gets old.* Seeing his arm around Marlise is becoming less shocking. I really should've predicted that. They say opposites attract, but there is no greater magnetic attraction than between two workaholics. Ask me how I know.

Only a stadium on gameday has ever had more football players in attendance. Oakley's mom brought the new man in her life. If Oakley had been worried about anyone announcing an engagement at her wedding reception, it would've been her mother. But even she's keeping the spotlight off herself tonight. Garth brought a date, and I have snapped so many candid shots of them, and he's going to love them. He can say it's a casual thing all he wants, but I know what I'm seeing when they look at each other.

After dancing to too many fast songs in a row with the most fun group of women here, I have to run to the table and shed my jacket. When I return to the floor, the next song is a slow one. Wick meets me as I head back to our table. He takes me in his arms and whispers, "I want to dance with my fiancée."

Fiancée. Wow. That's wild. I drape my arms around his neck. The ring has spun while I was getting sweaty out here, and I lift my hand and stare at it for a moment before I reach my thumb across to turn it back around. Two seconds of careless-ness. Her voice breaks through the music. "Nadine Mother-fucking Garrison!"

Her heels sound like thunder as she stomps toward us. She jerks my hand away from Wick's body. "Are you kidding me? Tonight? How could you?"

"I'm so sorry, Oakley. I swear I tried not to wear the ring until after your honeymoon but he begged me to leave it on and I was so torn but then your carriage was coming and . . ." *Why is she smiling? Why is he smiling?* "You knew. You were in on it?"

"Did you seriously think he picked that ring out all by himself? How could you think for a minute that I would be mad about this?"

The crowd that parted when she stormed over starts to clap as the dawning of what's happening hits them. "Come with me," she says, still grasping my hand.

"Where are we going?"

"To announce your engagement."

"We are not announcing anything. Go dance with your husband." She pulls harder than someone her size should be able to, leaving me no choice but to trail behind her.

We reach the DJ and she motions for him to stop the music. Then she motions for his microphone, and he hands it over with a smile, like he also knew this was going to happen.

"Everyone, may I have your attention please? We have a new reason to celebrate this evening." After a brief speech that makes me cry, she says the words, "Tonight, my best friend in the whole world accepted a ring from the only man who I've ever believed could handle her. Please raise your glasses to Nadine and Wick!"

Hollis whoops the loudest. Wick's eyes shine the brightest. And I am the absolute happiest I have ever been.

<<<>>>

ABOUT THE AUTHOR

Indie Sparks writes heroines with hutzpah and heroes with dirty mouths and the skills to walk the talk. She gives them all the happy endings they deserve, some for now, some forever. Spicy rom-coms are her favorite flavor in fiction. In real life, she favors the bold, wonderful tastes that some silly urban legend calls bitter and insists makes her more prone to becoming a serial unaliver. She wouldn't hurt anyone, but she would gladly take everyone's black coffee, red wine, and extra-dark chocolate. Her purse holds more lipsticks than money, and the only thing bulging more than her bookshelves is the men in her books.

ALSO BY INDIE SPARKS

MORE TITLES BY INDIE SPARKS

Peri

She was the wildest girl in town. He was the boy with the strongest arm and the truest aim. The rebel child and the golden boy. Together, they were hell-bent for chaos. Who was the match and who was the gasoline? Depended on the day. But that was a long time ago.

On My Merry Way

She may not have put "sexy stranger" on her Christmas list, but Santa knows what a good girl needs to make her holiday complete. Who knew one wrong-number text could turn out so right? Light the fireworks and pour the champagne! The naughty list is ready to make merry.

Modern Life of a Vintage Brat

She's an independent brat, who owns a vintage boutique. He's the smoking hot owner of the cigar bar next door, who is accustomed to being in control. She's not looking to be tamed, but she has no objection to him trying.

ALSO BY INDIE SPARKS

Steamy Rom-Com Duologies from INDIE SPARKS

VENGEFUL VIXENS:

Your Boss Says Hi!

She's only looking for a rebound guy, but her ex's boss plays for keeps. He's a former NFL player who used to have thousands of women screaming his name every week. Now, he only wants one woman to scream his name, and she just might become his biggest fan yet.

Your Trainer Says Hi!

(the book you just read)

NAUGHTY AT THE NOUVEAU:

Maintenance & Management

She's the new property manager. He's the new maintenance supervisor. They rub each other the wrong way . . . until they start to rub each other the right way. There's a non-fraternization policy, so they really shouldn't. But there's only one bed!

Landscaping & Leasing

He ghosted her after an unfortunate incident that she had absolutely no control over—and now, she's accidentally hired his landscaping company. She may not be completely immune to his charms (that voice!), but she's not weak enough to fall for him twice. But what if she doesn't know the whole story about why he disappeared from her life?

Milton Keynes UK
Ingram Content Group UK Ltd.
UKHW010653220124
436466UK00001B/66

9 798989 478033